THE
IDEAL
BAKERY

Stories by

DONALD
HALL

North Point Press
San Francisco
1987

Grateful acknowledgment is extended to
the publishers of earlier versions of these
stories: *The Georgia Review* ("The First
Woman," under the title "The World Is a
Bed"), *The New Yorker* ("Christmas
Snow"), *Esquire* ("The Fifty-Dollar Bill"
and "Mr. Schwartz"), *The Ohio Review*
("The Figure of the Woods" and "The Ideal
Bakery"), *Iowa Review* ("Widowers'
Woods" and "Revivals"), *Sewanee Review*
("Mrs. Thing"), *Antaeus* ("Argument and
Persuasion"), and *Ploughshares* ("Embar-
rassment").

For Tess and Ray

CONTENTS

THE
IDEAL
BAKERY

THE

FIRST

WOMAN

I.

William Bolter was thirty-two when he discovered that the world was a bed. If we lead a life of sexual excitement—as he thought—our lovers have had lovers and their lovers have had lovers also. Going to a revival of *West Side Story*, or to a gathering of the American Society of Statisticians, we see her; and we see *her*. We are episodes in the lives of each other, after all, and although we have not bedded down with X or Y or Z, we have had affairs with women who have had affairs with men who have had affairs with X and Y and Z. The world is a bed.

When an affair began, William liked to tell the story of the summer he was sixteen, and the first woman. Of course he could not simply blurt it out; no woman enjoyed the notion that she was one of a series. Yet he always wanted to tell the new woman about her predecessors—he reminded himself of obese people who spend dinnertime in anecdotes of famous meals—and he learned how to go about it: When alert skin subsided into mere dampness, when each leaned back to smoke, he would ask her, as if he stumbled on the thought, about the first time she had taken her clothes off for a man. Usually it was far enough back to be made light of. When she had finished her story he had license to tell his own.

2.

In June of 1945 Bill Bolter turned sixteen, a promising student of mathematics on a scholarship at Cranbrook Academy outside Detroit, and living with his parents. Besides mathematics there was the violin, dreams of composing and conducting, of becoming another Baumgartner to conduct his own compositions. He would have concentrated more on his music if he had not worried about the opinions of his classmates. With a diffidence common among adolescents—he told himself, when his old teacher sighed over his apostasy—he cared for the opinions of people dumber than he was; they accepted his presence when he swam a leg in a medley, but addressed him *Hey, fruit* when he walked with his violin past the Arts Academy, the Milles fountain, and the staid oaks, over the bright lawns to his teacher's quarters.

It was this diffidence that kept him from returning to the music camp at Interlochen where he had spent the previous two summers on a scholarship. This summer he practiced at home, continued his lessons, studied calculus in a desultory fashion, took a girl named Beverly to the movies, and read mystery stories. He was bored. When his mother told him about the chance to visit the Balfour Festival on Cape Cod, he was quick to take it.

Mrs. Hugh Fitzroberts, a large lady in her late forties, had befriended his mother in the thrift shop where his mother worked and had heard about William's musical abilities. Mrs.

Fitzroberts was wealthy, his mother told him, and a patron of the Detroit Symphony, some of whose members spent their summers in the blue air of Balfour. Her husband, on the other hand, was known to care more for balance sheets than for the finer things and would remain in Detroit aiding the war effort while Mrs. Fitzroberts rented a cabin with two bedrooms near the concert shell for the two weeks at the beginning of August, and it would be nice to have the boy for company.

They sat up all night on the coach to New York, the Wolverine, when not even the Fitzroberts name could swing a berth. At first the tall older lady attempted to interest him with intelligent questions, but after they had slept a few hours and awakened disheveled and grubby, their dignities fell away; Mrs. Fitzroberts became "Anne" and William "Bill," and they ate cheese sandwiches as dry as newsprint. At New York they made the connection to Boston where they transferred to a local, and as they approached the Cape her nervousness started. She became suddenly silly, he thought, skittish as a girl, reminding him of middle-aged men around soldiers—falsely friendly, laughing too much, guilty.

He discovered why. Waiting at the station was a ponderous man, older than she was, who occupied a chair in the Detroit Symphony hidden among woodwinds. They took each other's hands, and Mrs. Fitzroberts glanced back at her companion—her *cover*, he realized—with something like panic: There was something she had neglected to mention.

For the next fortnight, Bill saw little of Mrs. Fitzroberts, who never explained herself and never appeared at the cabin, and although he was shocked he was also pleased. It made him feel sophisticated; he found it a relief to be left alone in a new and handsome place with his music. In the mornings he practiced Beethoven, usually on a quiet patch of beach too rocky for bathing and out of range of sea salt. For a while even the natural world seemed to approve; the salt grass waved in his honor, and the cattails kept time like the batons of a thousand conductors. Afternoons he attended rehearsals of the visiting quartet—they were working through Beethoven, as it happened—and daydreamed himself a great performer. At night there were concerts in the shell near his cabin.

And there were girls—dozens of young women and few young men. Girls waited on table, flocked together in boarding houses, played flutes and violas, took notes during rehearsals. Most of them were older than he was—eighteen, twenty, twenty-three. He walked in a grove of young women, lush and warm and possible. He had lunch with one girl, went to a rehearsal with another, ate supper with another, took a fourth to the concert and afterwards walked the beach with her and kissed. To each of the girls he pleaded his plea of bed. A few of them confessed to being virgins like him; others warded him off lightly. He suspected that they felt awkward about taking a sixteen-year-old seriously. And when each of them refused his proposal, Bill was quick to abandon her, for it meant he could pay suit to another. Every night he went home feeling rejected and relieved.

There was no competition at all. The only young men at Balfour at the end of the war were crippled or homosexual. (Bill discouraged the attentions of a thirty-year-old piano teacher.) So he dated a girl with a good figure and big teeth who played the cello. He swam on a Sunday with a bank president's daughter, and with a Smith graduate he drank illicit beer in a coupe she was driving while her brother was in Europe. For a time he lost interest in music: He was too tired in the mornings to practice. Yet after ten days of frantic dating he had not gone to bed with anyone. When he caught sight of Mrs. Fitzroberts, looking younger every day, irony saturated him.

Slowly he became aware of the girl in the red MG. Not many students had brought cars to Balfour, because of gas rationing. On the one night in the coupe, he and the Smith girl counted the miles that they drove. But the tall black-haired young woman whirled in her red MG through the small streets, parking beside the only expensive restaurant in town. Several of the girls mentioned her, annoyed at the ubiquity of the red MG. Then late one morning—Balfour almost done—he paused when the MG parked at the tennis court near where he walked. The tall girl leapt out and took up singles with an older woman who clerked at the hotel. The girl wore a short tennis dress, the skirt fluted like a Greek column, and her legs were long, smooth, strong, luxurious. She leaned forward to wait for service with an intensity that looked omnivorous.

The next day he came to the tennis court at the same time and brought a racquet and hit balls against the backboard while the girl with the red MG played tennis with the older woman. When they finished and her companion walked away toward the hotel, he approached the tall girl. She smiled at him, and he noticed the wedding ring, and he asked her if she would like to practice with him; when they were tired she drove him back to his room. He asked her if she would play again tomorrow, and she asked him about his music, and she told him that her name was Margaret Adams Olson but everyone called her Mitsy. Her husband, Allen, was an army captain in the Pacific, Intelligence, and she was twenty-four. She came from Seattle, and after the war she and Allen would settle nearby in Allison— "like June Allyson with an *i*"—where the Olsons owned the bank, which was like owning the town. Her music was strictly amateur, she said. She was here because she was bored.

The next day they played and had lunch and met for the Mozart at night and afterwards walked on the beach and talked. He asked her how she had gas for her car and she laughed and showed him a wad of A coupons clutched in an elastic band; her father took care of that. If your husband was overseas, Mitsy said, and there was nothing to do, why not have some fun? Last year had been rotten, really rotten, she said, because her great-aunt was sick with cancer, right in their house, and they had to take care of her until she died. Then she told him about her husband, and their courtship in college, and how her husband was a dilettante at the piano, and they had met at a concert, a soprano visiting Seattle, she couldn't remember which one. And all the time she talked, animated and charming, he thought only of thighs blooming beneath a white linen skirt.

Gulls flew in circles over their heads; he squinted to watch them as they circled and imagined for the moment that the gulls were spying on them.

Bill asked her if there had been other boyfriends, wanting to keep her close to the subject, and Mitsy laughed as she told him: Yes, yes, that was what she had lived for at college—because her father had always been too busy to pay attention to her—and really she had been terrible. She had been cheerleader her freshman year because it was a way to meet upperclassmen and football players, and for her first three years she had dated every night, somebody different every night. She was booked for dates three weeks ahead—she told him, and her eyes were brilliant—and on weekends she had two dates a day. Sometimes three.

He felt embarrassed that she might see the effect her words had.

The day before the festival ended, they played tennis again, the third day in a row. For two nights he had slept irregularly, but conjured up her strong, firm, welcoming body, and then drifted off into small patches of sleep, only to wake dreaming erotic dreams. Today again Mitsy wore the fluted white tennis dress, and Bill was so full of her he could not play at all. He was lovesick, he told himself, "sick with longing." After a set that he lost 6–0, she asked him if he was not feeling well, and he agreed that he was not, and they drove together in the red

MG back to her hotel. In the lobby everyone scurried about, looking serious and giddy at the same time. They would have lunch after Mitsy changed her clothes. As they waited for the elevator, they heard the hotel's PA system telling them that, on account of the surrender of the Japanese, the evening Shostakovich and Prokofiev had been canceled, replaced by a ceremony of memorial and celebration.

He felt shocked—as if Captain Olson might walk through the door and take her away from him. She was jumping beside him, saying, "Allen! Allen!"; and then she dropped her tennis racquet, hugged him, and kissed him on the mouth. And before she let him go and fell back laughing, he felt with astonishment her tongue push through his lips and twist for a moment against his tongue. Then the elevator took her away.

At lunch they decided that the memorial service was not for them. They listened to the gaiety around them and felt separate from it. "They don't really mean it," Mitsy said.

He was scornful. "They've seen movies of Armistice Day."

She suggested they have a picnic on the beach, in celebration. She would collect a basket of food, and tonight while the other people were at their service, they would sit on the beach and drink wine.

She picked him up at five. His heart pounded as he sat beside her, sneaking looks downward where her gray slacks tucked inside her thighs and made a V. She had visited the delicatessen, bought cold chicken, pâté, tomatoes, cole slaw, potato salad, and wine—two bottles of prewar French wine; he tried to memorize the label, but the French dissolved when he looked away from it.

Bill sat near her on the blanket, and in a moment her knee was touching his thigh, and he could feel nothing else. She opened the wine, and out of Dixie Cups they toasted the end of the war. They nibbled at this and that, then confessed that neither of them felt hungry. After a pause in the conversation, after a drink that inaugurated their second bottle, he said, "You know all those dates, all those boys at college . . . "

He waited so long without continuing his question that she said, "Yes?"

" . . . did you sleep with them?" he asked. When he heard himself he felt how naive he sounded.

Mitsy laughed. "Not with all of them, Bill," she said. "Not even with many of them. Some. A few."

He felt jealousy rise in him. "Didn't your husband mind?"

"He was one of them," she said. "He went with other girls, too. Why are you asking me?" she said. She sounded friendly.

"Because I want to go to bed with you, too," he said.

She patted his shoulder and smiled pleasantly. "But I can't," she said, "because I'm married and I love my husband."

"I'm a virgin," he said. He felt himself looking depressed. "I'll get a whore."

"Don't do that," she said. "Don't be silly. There are lots of girls who would sleep with you. I'd love to, except for being married, I mean happily married."

Bill fell silent then, with anguish; and alongside the anguish he felt something like cunning. He dropped his head on his chest. He heard her take another swallow from her Dixie Cup. Then Mitsy swiveled toward him on the blanket. He felt her arm extend around his shoulders, squeezing. He still looked down, keeping his eyes closed. Then her finger lifted his chin, and he felt her lips on his. This time her tongue went in his mouth right away, and stayed there, and he felt his penis rise rigid against his tight underpants and his khaki trousers. With his hand he touched her breast, or the sweater over her breast, and she moaned and moved so that their thighs pressed against each other.

"I can't," she said. "I can't. Not now."

He said nothing but put his tongue in her mouth.

As they kissed, her hand swept slowly from his knee to his shoulder, pausing near his waist. Then her hand squeezed him through his clothing.

"Oh, God," she said. "I give up. Come on. Come back to the room."

That was all there was, when William told the story later, except for the things that she said, lying with him on top of the sheets in her room. "It's all right," Mitsy said, "because I love Allen so much." And when they first touched, naked, leg to leg, thigh to thigh, breast to breast, her long hair dangling against his shoulder she said, "This is your first time. Feel it— the *skin*."

The next day Mrs. Fitzroberts appeared again, looking slimmer and younger and not formidable at all, and wept, packing her bags. He should be weeping also—he thought to himself—but when he tried looking morose he felt silly and broke out in a grin. He hinted to Mrs. Fitzroberts about what had happened, and she patted his shoulder. She said that love was the most important thing in the world—the only thing. As they waited on the porch for the taxi that would take them to the station, among crowds of other visitors standing in front of cabins with suitcases, he wondered how many of them had risen from quick beds. Then a red MG swooped down the road, as he had expected it to, and Mitsy leapt out, shining and untouched, and kissed him long and hard, in front of all the people, then drove away, and he did not see her again for thirty-five years.

3.

In 1965, in early autumn, William went to a cocktail party in Manhattan. He had lived there a dozen years, teaching mathematics to graduate engineers, with a specialty that earned him consultancy fees. His host introduced him to a Mrs. Dodge, the host's sister, and Mrs. Dodge answered his routine question by saying that she lived in Allison, Washington.

He asked her if she was acquainted with a Mrs. Allen Olson.

Mrs. Dodge's smile turned artificial. "Yes," she said, "but I'm afraid she's too grand for me." They both laughed, and his host interrupted and introduced Mrs. Dodge to someone else.

So Mrs. Dodge was jealous of her. On the twenty-year-old snapshot of Mitsy Olson, clear in memory, he tried to impose various "too grand" enlargements, a gallery of Helen Hokinson ladies. None of the images endured. From time to time, over twenty years, he had been curious to see her; now he felt the curiosity again. How strange to hear of her a continent away twenty years later. But the world is a bed, he reminded himself. He had encountered again a woman of the past; it made a connection even with Mrs. Dodge.

At this time in his life everything that happened seemed to make such a connection. William had married in his senior year at Michigan, too young, and had remained faithful for five years, doing his Ph.D. and beginning to teach. Then there was an episode with a graduate student, and another with a colleague's wife met at a conference. For a year or two he hurtled from affair to affair—inventing late department meetings, conference weekends, Saturday committees—and gradually realized the grandeur of sexual association. He shuffled in the giant dance, and mathematics suffered, but he had known for some years that he would never be more than competent. And music, which his wife did not enjoy, dwindled to an excuse for absence: He went so far as to invent a string quartet in Detroit that practiced Wednesday evenings, often until two or three in the morning.

This extravagance was interrupted when he fell in love, divorced his wife, and married again—for six months—a young woman he loved and could not abide. When he divorced again he took his job in New York. Cautious of love, finding comfort in variety, he lived in his flat on Ninth Street a life of promiscuous harmony—revisiting old girls sometimes, always with two or three to telephone if he was lonesome—and he searched continually at parties, in bars, at concerts, at the Museum of Modern Art, for the faces of women he would add to his long encounter, as they added him to their own. And many times, as he lay in bed with a new woman, the light from Fifth Avenue faint through the curtains, he told them stories of his sexual life and sought from them stories of their own. He told about his initiation at Balfour, and the first woman whose skin he had touched.

Tonight he glanced over the party to assess the crowd, then moved from group to group with his glass, drinking little, listening to conversations. There was a pretty blonde woman, early thirties, with the animation of the newly divorced. He passed her over; he wanted no tears. There was a young woman, beautiful if overly made-up, surrounded by a shifting group of males and no women at all. Someone identified her vaguely familiar face; she reported local television news and was supposed to graduate to a network. There would be no tears with that one . . . but there would be nothing else either. The men would mill about her all night, making little jousts of jokes and attention, and at some point she would glance at her watch, speak of a morning deadline, and disappear, leaving the men to each other. William found himself seeking out a tall and pleasant young woman, long legs and large glasses, pretty hair, who was eager to laugh with him. After half an hour of talk, he suggested that she find her purse. She did not protest.

As they were leaving he looked for his host and found him standing with Mrs. Dodge, who was very drunk. "Your banker's bitch," she said to William, twisting the word, "—no one is good enough for her. Holier than thou. I wish she'd fall off that deck and break her goddamned neck."

4.

In 1980, at fifty-one, he looked forty, they told him, and when he shaved each morning he tested the flattery out. Although his hair was thin, it was black, and he had grown a burly mustache; with handball and diet his waistline remained what it had been at sixteen. His life had not noticeably altered for twenty years, and he took pride in his life, especially as he saw his friends turn fat, alcoholic, diabetic, frightened, and old; one or two had had the bad luck to die. It was true that sometimes he was bored. It was true that the prospect of old age depressed him, and when he allowed it to surface, loneliness felt heavy in his chest. It was true that his love affairs, which he continued to enjoy, had become repetitious. William boasted to his male acquaintances that he had discovered a three-part solution, a relationship partaking of music at its most mathematical. In this solution he kept one love affair beginning, one at a summery peak of attention, and one diminishing into silence. The trick was never to allow two to occupy the same phase, or to allow any moment without resource.

It was boredom, not need for money, that led him impulsively to accept a summer teaching job at the University of Washington. Within a week he had found a young woman who moved in with him for the summer, perhaps a dangerous departure from his three-part invention, but undertaken with forethought. He had begun to suspect that he would marry again—perhaps at sixty, perhaps even closer to retirement. And he had not lived with a woman for twenty-odd years.

Two weeks after his arrival, he found Allison on the map, and on a free Friday morning drove for an hour past hills and rivers and waterfalls through great stands of timber. For the first time in years he felt dazzled by the natural world, almost elated with the grandeur of vista and swoop. Maybe this joy was a good omen for his journey. He reminded himself that returns were always foolish—Mitsy might not be there, might not even be alive—but he *was* curious. The girl in the red MG, the first woman of his life, the social snob of 1965—he speculated on what he would find. He would find a woman fifty-nine years old! Then he remembered his own age, and the boredom of his present life made him shudder as he drove. Perhaps he was coming to the end of a thirty-five-year adventure; how appropriate, then, to revisit the first woman.

He entered the streets of the small town, *Class of 80* spray-painted on the watertower, and found the name listed in the phone book. When he telephoned from the drugstore, a maid's voice told him that Mrs. Olson was out but expected home soon. William represented himself as an old friend who preferred not to leave his name because he wanted to surprise Mrs. Olson. He took directions, parked beside a redwood carport, and walked past a border of irises toward the low modern house. His heart pounded as he rang the bell in the bright morning. Mrs. Olson was changing her clothes, and he waited in a large Japanese living room. Long windows gave onto a deck that looked down a gully to a stream. There was money in the room, well employed and inconspicuous. Three paintings on the wall were signed with a name he could not read.

When she walked in, he entertained for a moment the illusion that she had not changed at all. She stood straight and firm, her black hair tied back. Then he saw, as if a film pulled away and he looked behind it, that her face was everywhere finely wrinkled, with dark creases under her eyes and at the sides of her mouth and a trembling looseness under her chin. She was fifty-nine—and remarkable. Her hair was dyed and her figure was trim, her legs a little knobbed with veins faintly blue under her tan. She reminded him, in fact, of Mrs. Fitzroberts.

"Yes?" she was saying. She looked at him firmly, *grand*.

"William Bolter," he mumbled, and gave her his hand. "We knew each other in 1945," he said. "At Balfour. When you had the red MG. . . . We played tennis." She looked as if she were trying to remember. He kept on: "V-J Day, Mitsy."

"Oh," she said, and looked pleased, and then flushed lightly with a look that he remembered. "No one calls me that now," she laughed. "*Margaret*," she pronounced, mocking her own dignity. "I've thought about you. I've wondered so often what . . . My goodness!" She laughed, and again thirty-five years disappeared for a moment. "Really," she said, "I didn't think you would remember me."

He laughed. "Of course I remember you, and I remember June Allyson."

He told her what he was doing in Seattle, and that he had abandoned the violin because you could not serve two masters, and he told her how remarkably unchanged she was. She told him about her life in Allison, about her two grown children, a granddaughter. There was a child who had died. She told about a return to Balfour, the changes there, not for the better. . . . She gave him sherry. She would like him to meet her husband, she said, but he would not be home until late; would he please stay for lunch? She left the room to speak with the cook.

When she returned he asked her, "Who did the paintings?"

She looked pleased again. "Gilbert Honiger," she said. "He's a friend of ours. He lives on a farm west of here." She refilled their sherry glasses. He told her about meeting the woman from Allison at the New York party, without repeating the conversation, and she wrinkled her nose faintly when he pronounced Mrs. Dodge's name. Fair's fair, he thought. He liked her style better than Mrs. Dodge's.

Then he began to reminisce about the old summer, and she

seemed happy to join in. He remarked that, over the years, he had come to think that artistic festivals had as much to do with art as checker tournaments did. He was going to tell an anecdote about a Balfour conductor, but she interrupted. "That's what Gilbert says," she said, and made a gesture toward the paintings. "He went to Santa Cruz one summer for something and walked out on the second day." The delighted look was on her face again—and he knew that Gilbert was her lover, and felt a regret he could not justify.

Lunch was an omelette with Grey Riesling and a salad. They talked lightly and it was pleasant but he began to feel irritation and loss. He mocked himself for expecting grand opera. They emptied the bottle of wine and she pressed a buzzer on the floor and the maid brought another. He drank several glasses. He spoke lightly of his two marriages. Feeling mildly flirtatious, he let her know that he had not lost interest in young women; he mentioned the girl in Seattle, who was twenty-four.

He noticed that she had stopped drinking; he kept on. Annoyed that she revealed less than he did, he talked without pausing. He had kept up with contemporary music, and liked it; she had followed it less, she said, and didn't like what she heard. He found himself lecturing, as if he were in a classroom, and the more pompous he knew he sounded, the less he could stop, while her smile grew fainter and more distant. He began to feel angry with her, this smooth social creature, Margaret not Mitsy, who had once clutched him on a beach in Massachusetts. Irritated, he began to be insulting about people who were unable to hear anything later than Stravinsky, and he watched her smile turn cold.

Then again he saw through her dyed hair, back to the luxurious twenty-four-year-old hair of 1945, spread on the pillow of her hotel room the night they stayed together. He wanted urgently to be closer to her, to force her to acknowledge that old closeness, to break through the light graceful surface that she wore to protect herself. Yes, he wanted to make love to her again, and he thought of pulling her up from her relaxed chair and kissing her. Instead, he said, "Gilbert is your lover."

"What?" she said. He watched her cheeks grow red.

"Gilbert is your lover," he said. "The world is a bed. Everybody is everybody's lover. What does it matter? It doesn't matter." When he saw her flush he realized that he was drunk and babbling. "I mean—," he stumbled on, "it's none of my business what you do; I mean I understand. . . . The world is a bed."

She was looking down at her plate. After a pause she said, "If Betty Dodge told you that she is a liar. . . . "

He shook his head. "She didn't say. I understand about these things."

She laughed. "You understand. . . . Why do you say something so stupid? I haven't seen you for thirty-five years and I've been perfectly decent to you. Gilbert is homosexual and has lived with someone named Harold for twenty years. Harold is dying now. I spent the morning with him. . . . It was such a beautiful morning. Maybe you noticed . . . if you notice anything. I sat in the bedroom with Harold who didn't even know I was there and watched the sunlight coming through an oak Gilbert transplanted there twenty years ago. The sunlight kept getting into Harold's eyes and bothering him until I pulled the shade. What do you *understand*?"

A sense of his own ridiculousness rose to his cheeks and burned below his eyes. "Oh," he said. "Oh . . . I'm sorry . . . It was foolish . . . I was trying . . . " He could not think how to explain.

"*The world is a bed*," she quoted. "That's what you like to say, isn't it? Of course it is. The world is a bed and someone is always dying in it. Have you ever sat with someone dying? My daughter died when she was sixteen."

"I'm sorry," he said. He stood up. "I'm very sorry. I hate to be stupid. . . . "

"I suppose that changed my life more than anything else did." She stood up also. "But most people turn more serious when they get older. . . . " She looked past him out the windows where the deck hung over the gully. He understood that she was no longer addressing him. "But some people stay children and when they die they are still children. Harold was like that."

"I'm sorry," he said again, "I'm sorry." Then, as if it would explain things, he blurted, "You were the first woman I ever made love to."

"And you were the last man I went to bed with," she said, "except for my husband. Oh, you idiot. You were a sixteen-year-old boy named Bill, sweet, and I was lonesome. I suppose I used you to make myself feel powerful the way I did at college . . . and for you of course I was a prize to bring back to school, like a trophy you won swimming. But you were decent enough back then. Now you are an old fool full of self-regard because you still take young women to bed with you. What a life."

He left quickly then.

Two horses stood nose to tail under a live oak, unmoving in late afternoon sun, in the gully below his car. As he drove to Seattle in gathering dusk, fuzzy with wine, he tried to concentrate on the road and on route signs, but waves of dismay rose over him like nausea. Back at the apartment he fixed himself a whiskey and quarreled with the young woman who lived with him. Twenty-four hours later she departed weeping and carrying two suitcases. When relief rolled over him, he knew that his petulance had served some purpose; his mood immediately lightened, shifting to anticipation: On the floor above him lived a redheaded instructor in physical education—with a child, but no husband in evidence—whose muscular calves he admired when they nodded to each other by the mailbox.

CHRISTMAS

SNOW

The real snows I remember are the snows of Christmas in New Hampshire. I was ten years old, and there was a night when I woke up to the sound of grown-ups talking. Slowly, I realized that it wasn't that at all; the mounds of my grandfather and grandmother lay still in their bed under many quilts in the cold room. It was rain falling and rubbing against the bushes outside my window. I sat up in bed, pulling the covers around me, and held the green shade out from the frosty pane. There were flakes of snow mixed into the rain—large, slow flakes fluttering down like wet leaves. I watched as long as I could, until the back of my neck hurt with the cold, while the flakes grew thicker and the snow took over the rain. When I looked up into the dark sky, just before lying back in my warm feather bed, the whole air was made of fine light shapes. I was happy in my own world of snow, as if I were living inside one of those glass paperweights that snow when you shake them, and

I went back to sleep easily. In the morning, I looked out the window as soon as I woke. There were no more leaves, no more weeds turned brown by the frost, no sheds, no road, and no chicken coops. The sky was a dense mass of snowflakes, the ground covered in soft white curves.

It was the morning of Christmas Eve, 1938. The day before, we had driven north from Connecticut, and I had been disappointed to find that there was no snow on my grandfather's farm. On the trip up, I had not noticed the lack of snow because I was too busy looking for hurricane damage. (September 1938 was the time of the great New England hurricane.) Maples and oaks and elms were down everywhere. Huge roots stood up like dirt cliffs next to the road. On distant hillsides, whole stands of trees lay pointing in the same direction, like combed hair. Men were cutting the timber with double handsaws, their breaths blue-white in the cold. Ponds were already filling with logs—stored timber that would corduroy the surface of New Hampshire lakes for years. Here and there I saw a roof gone from a barn, or a tree leaning into a house.

We knew from letters that my grandfather's farmhouse was all right. I was excited to be going there, sitting in the front seat between my mother and father, with the heater blasting at my knees. Every summer we drove the same route and I spent two weeks following my grandfather as he did chores, listening to his talk. The familiar road took shape again: Sunapee, Georges Mills, New London; then there was the shortcut along the bumpy Cilleyville Road. We drove past the West Andover depot, past Henry's store and the big rock, and climbed the little hill by the Blasington's, and there, down the slope to the right, we saw the lights of the farmhouse. In a porch window I could see my small Christmas tree, with its own string of lights. It stood in the window next to the large one, where I could see it when we drove over the hill.

We stopped in the driveway and the kitchen door loosened a

wedge of yellow light. My grandfather stood in his milking clothes, tall and bald and smiling broadly. He lifted me up, grunting at how big I was getting. Over his shoulder, which smelled happily of barn and tie-up, I saw my grandmother in her best dress, waiting her turn and looking pleased.

As we stood outside in the cold, I looked around for signs of the hurricane. In the light from the kitchen window I could just see a stake with a rope tied to it that angled up into the tall maple by the shed. Then I remembered that my grandmother had written my mother about that tree. It had blown over, roots out of the ground, and Washington Woodward, a cousin of ours who lived on Ragged Mountain, was fixing it. The great tree was upright now.

My grandfather saw me looking at it. "Looks like it's going to work, don't it? Of course you can't tell until spring, and the leaves. A lot of the root must have gone." He shook his head. "Wash is a wonder," he said. "He winched that tree back upright in two days with a pulley on that oak." He pointed to a tree on the hill in back of the house. "I thought he was going to pull that oak clear out of the ground. Then he took that rock-moving machine of his" (I remembered that Wash had constructed a wooden tripod about fifteen feet high for moving rocks. I never understood how it worked, though I heard him explain it a hundred times. He moved rocks for fun mostly; it was his hobby) "and moved that boulder down from the pasture and set it there to keep the roots flat. It only took him five days in all, and I think he saved the tree."

It was when we moved back to the group around the car that I realized, with sudden disappointment, that there was no snow on the ground.

I turned from the window the next morning and looked over at my grandparents' bed. My grandmother was there, but the place beside her was empty. The clock on the bureau, among snapshots and perfume bottles, said six o'clock. I heard my grandfather carrying wood into the living room. Logs crashed into the big, square stove. In a moment I heard another sound I had been listening for—a massive animal roar from the same stove. He had poured a tin can of kerosene on the old embers and the new logs. Then I heard him fix the kitchen stove and pause by the door to put on coats and scarves and a cap—his boots were in the shed—and then the door shut between kitchen and shed, and he had gone to milk the cows.

It was warm inside my bed. My grandmother stood up beside her bed, her gray hair down to her waist. "Good morning," she said. "You awake? We've had some snow. You go back to sleep while I make the doughnuts." That brought me out of bed quickly. I dressed next to the stove in the dark living room. The sides of the stove glowed red, and I kept my distance. The cold of the room almost visibly receded into the farther corners, there to dwindle into something the size of a pea.

My grandmother was fixing her hair in the warm kitchen, braiding it and winding it up on her head. She looked like my grandmother again. "Doughnuts won't be ready for a long time. Fat's got to heat. Why don't you have a slice of bread and go see Gramp in the tie-up?"

I put peanut butter on the bread and bundled up with galoshes and a wool cap that I could pull over my ears. I stepped outside into the swirl of flakes, white against the gray of the early morning. It was my first snow of the year, and it set my heart pounding with pleasure. But even if it had snowed in Connecticut earlier, this would have been my first real snow. When it snowed in Connecticut, the snowplows heaped most of it in the gutters and the cars chewed the rest with chains and blackened it with oil. Here the snow turned the farm into a planet of its own, an undiscovered moon.

I walked past our Studebaker, which was humped already

with two inches of snow. I reached down for a handful, to see if it would pack, but it was dry as cotton. The flakes, when I looked up into the endless flaking barrel of the sky, were fine and constant. It was going to snow all day. I climbed the hill to the barn without lifting my galoshes quite clear of the snow and left two long trenches behind me. I raised the iron latch and went into the tie-up, shaking my head and shoulders like a dog, making a little snowstorm inside.

My grandfather laughed. "It's really coming down," he said. "It'll be a white Christmas, you can be sure of that."

"I love it," I said.

"Can you make a snowman today?"

"It's dry snow," I said. "It won't pack."

"When it melts a little, you can roll away the top of it—I mean, tomorrow or the next day. I remember making a big one with my brother Fred when I was nine—no, eight. Fred wasn't much bigger than a hoptoad then. I called him Hoptoad when I wanted to make him mad, and my, you never saw such a red face. Well, we spent the whole day Saturday making this great creature. Borrowed a scarf and an old hat—it was a woman's hat, but we didn't mind—and a carrot from the cellar for the nose, and two little potatoes for the eyes. It was a fine thing, no doubt about it, and we showed your Aunt Lottie, who said it was the best one she ever saw. Then my father came out of the forge—putting things away for the Sabbath, you know, shutting things away—and he saw what we'd been up to and came over and stood in front of it. I can see him now, so tall, with his big brown beard. We were proud of that snowman, and I guess we were waiting for praise. 'Very good, boys,' he said." Here my grandfather's voice turned deep and impressive. " 'That's a fine snowman. It's too bad you put him in front of the shed. You can take him down now.' " My grandfather laughed. "Of course, we felt bad, but we felt silly, too. The back of that snowman was almost touching the carriage we drove to church in. We were tired with making it, and I guess we were tired when we came in for supper! I suppose that was the last snowman I ever made."

I loved him to tell his stories. His voice filled the white-washed, cobwebby tie-up. I loved his imitations, and the glimpses of an old time. In this story I thought my great-grandfather sounded cruel; there must have been some *other* way to get to church. But I didn't really care. I never really got upset by my grandfather's stories, no matter what happened in them. All the characters were fabulous, and none more so than his strong blacksmith father, who had fought at Vicksburg.

My grandfather was milking now, not heavily dressed against the cold but most of the time wedged between the bodies of two huge holsteins, which must have given off a good bit of heat. The alternate streams of milk went swush-swush from his fists into the pail, first making a tinny sound and then softening and becoming more liquid as the pail filled. When he wasn't speaking, he leaned his head on the rib cage of a cow, the visor of his cap turned around to the back like a baseball catcher's. When he spoke, he tilted his head back and turned toward me. He sat on an old easy chair with the legs cut off, while I had taken down a three-legged stool from a peg on the wall. We talked about the hurricane a bit, and he made jokes about "Harry Cane" and "Si Clone." Whenever the pail was full, he would take it to the milk room and strain it into the big milk can, which the truck would pick up later in the day. We went from cow to cow, from Sally to Spot to Betty to Alice Weaver. And then we were done. While the last milk strained into the big can, I helped my grandfather clean out the tie-up, hoeing the cowflops through the floor and onto the manure heap under the barn. Then he fitted tops on the milk cans and craned them onto his wheelbarrow. I unlatched the door and we went out into the snow.

The trenches that I had scraped with my galoshes were filled in. The boulder that Washington Woodward had rolled over the roots of the maple wore a thick white cap; it looked like an enormous snowball. The air was a chaff of white motes, the tiny dry flakes. (I remembered last summer in the barn, sneezing with the fine dust while my grandfather pitched hay.) The iron wheel of the wheelbarrow made a narrow cut in the snow and spun a long delicate arc of snow forward. Our four boots made a new trail. Crossing the road to the platform on the other side, we hardly knew where the road began and the ditch ended. We were all alone, with no trace of anything else in the world. We came back to the kitchen for breakfast, slapping our hands and stamping our feet, exhilarated with cold and with the first snow of the winter.

I smelled the doughnuts when we opened the door from the shed to the kitchen. My father was standing in the kitchen, wearing a light sweater over an open-neck shirt, smoking his before-breakfast cigarette. On the stove, the fat was bubbling, and I could see the circles of dough floating and turning brown. When she saw me, my grandmother tossed a few more doughnuts into the fat, and I watched them greedily as they floated among the bubbles. In a moment, my mother came downstairs, and we all ate doughnuts and drank milk and coffee.

"Is it going to snow all day?" my father asked my grandfather.

"It looks so," said my grandfather.

"I hope the girls can get through," said my grandmother. She always worried about things. My mother's schoolteacher sisters were expected that night.

"They will, Katie," said my grandfather.

"They have chains, I suppose," said my father.

"Oh, yes," said my grandfather, "and they're good drivers."

"Who else is coming?" I asked.

"Uncle Luther," said my grandfather, "and Wash. Wash will have to find his way down Ragged."

That morning after breakfast, my Aunt Caroline arrived, and before noon my Aunt Nan. Each of them talked with me for a while, and then each of them was absorbed by the kitchen and preparations for tomorrow's dinner. I kept looking at the presents under both trees—a pile for the grown-ups under the branches of the big tree, and almost as many under mine. After lunch, Nan drove up to "Sabine," Uncle Luther's small house a quarter of a mile north, and brought him back. He was my grandmother's older brother, a clergyman who had retired from his city parish and was preaching at the little South Danbury church that we went to in New Hampshire. My grandfather disappeared for a while—nobody would tell me where he was—and a little later my grandmother was plucking feathers from a hen named Old Rusty that had stopped laying eggs. Then my grandfather dressed up in a brown suit, because it was Christmas Eve, and read a novel by Kathleen Norris. My father read magazines or paced up and down with a cigarette. I must have seemed restless, because after a while my father plucked one of my presents from under my tree and told me to open it. It was a Hardy Boys mystery. I sat in the living room with my father and grandfather and read a Christmas book.

By four-thirty, it was perfectly dark, and the snow kept coming. When I looked out the sitting-room window, past the light the windows cast into the front yard, I saw darkness with shadows of snow upon it. Inside the cup of light, the snow floated like feathers. It piled high on the little round stones on each side of the path from the driveway. Farther on in the darkness I could see the dark toadstool of the birdbath weighted down under an enormous puff of whiteness. I went to the kitchen window to look at our car, but there was only a car-shaped drift of snow, with indentations for the windows.

It was time for milking again. My grandfather bundled up with extra socks and sweaters and scarves, and long boots over his suit trousers, and my grandmother pinned his coat around his neck with a huge safety pin. She always fretted about his health. She had also been fretting for an hour over Washington Woodward. (Wash had been sort of an older brother to her when she was a little girl; his family had been poor and had farmed him out to the Keneston cousins.) My grandfather stepped out the shed door and sank into the snow. He started to take big steps toward the barn when suddenly he stopped and we heard him shout, "Katie, Donnie, look!" Peering out the shed window, we could just see my grandfather in the reflected light from the kitchen. He was pointing past that light, and while we watched, a figure moved into it, pacing slowly with a shuffling sort of gait. Then the figure said, "Wesley!" and started talking, and we knew it was Wash.

It would have been hard to tell what it was if it hadn't talked. Wash looked as if he was wearing six coats, and the outermost was the pelt of a deer. He shot one every winter and dried its pelt on the side of his hut; I think the pelts served to keep out the wind, for one thing. His face was almost covered with horizontal strips of brown cloth, covered with snow now, leaving just a slit for the eyes. The same sort of strips, arranged vertically, fastened his cap to his head and tied under his chin.

When he shuffled up to the shed door, my grandmother opened it. "Snowshoes," she said. "I knew that's how you'd do it, maybe." She laughed—with relief I suppose, and also at Wash's appearance. Wash was talking, of course—he was always talking—but I didn't notice what he said. I was too busy watching him take off his snowshoeing clothes. First, standing in the doorway but still outside, he stripped three gloves from each hand and tossed them ahead of him into the shed. It was even cold for us to stand watching him in the open door, but Wash had to take off his snowshoes before he could come inside. His thick, cold fingers fumbled among leather thongs. Finally, he stood out of them, banged them against the side of the house to shake the snow off them, and stepped inside. As we closed the shed door, I saw my grandfather trudge up the blue hill toward the barn.

A single naked light bulb burned at the roof of the shed. Wash stamped his feet and found his gloves and put them on a table. All the time, his voice went on and on. "About there, McKenzie's old place, my left shoe got loose. I had to stop there by the big rock and fix it. It took me a while, because I didn't have a good place to put my foot. Well, I was standing there pretty quiet, getting my breath, when a red fox came sniffing along. . . ."

Now he began taking off the layers of his clothing. He unknotted the brown bands around his face, and they turned into long socks. "How do you like these, Katie?" he interrupted himself. "You gave them to me last Christmas, and I hain't worn them yet." He went on with his story. When all the socks were peeled off, they revealed his beard. Beards were rare in 1938. I saw a few in New Hampshire, usually on old men. Washington shaved his beard every spring and grew it again in the fall, so I knew two Washington Woodwards—the summer one and the winter one. The beard was brown-gray, and it served him most of the winter instead of a scarf. It was quite full already and it wagged as he talked. His eyes crinkled in the space left between the two masses of his beard and his hair. Wash never cut his hair in winter, either—also for the sake of warmth. He thought we should use the hair God gave us before we went to adding other things.

He unwound himself now, taking off the pelt of the deer, which was frozen and stiff, and then a series of coats and jackets. Then there was a pair of overalls, and then I saw that he had wrapped burlap bags around his shins and thighs, underneath the legs of the overalls, and tied them in place with bits of string. It took him a long time to undo the knots, but he refused to cut them away with a knife; that would have been a waste. Then he was down to his boots, his underneath overalls, his old much-mended shirt, and a frail brown cardigan over it. He took off his boots, and we walked through the kitchen and into the living room.

Everyone welcomed Wash, and we heard him tell about his four-hour walk down Ragged on snowshoes, about the red fox and the car he saw abandoned. "Come to think of it," my father said, "I haven't heard any traffic going past."

Wash interrupted his own monologue. "Nothing can get through just now. It's a bad storm. I suppose Benjamin's plow broke down again. Leastways we're all here for the night."

"Snowbound," said my Uncle Luther.

"Got the wood in?" Washington asked my grandfather.

Aunt Nan recited:

> Shut in from all the world without,
> We sat the clean-winged hearth about,
> Content to let the north-wind roar
> In baffled rage at pane and door,
> While the red logs before us beat
> The frost-line back with tropic heat . . .

She giggled when she was through.

Aunt Caroline said, "I remember when we had to learn that."

"Miss Headley," my mother said. She turned to me. "Do you have that in school? It's John Greenleaf Whittier, 'Snow-Bound.'"

"Are we really snowbound?" I said. I liked the idea of it. I felt cozy and protected, walled in by the snow. I wanted it to keep on snowing all winter, so that I wouldn't have to go back to Connecticut and school.

"If we have to get out, we'll get out," my father said quickly.

In a moment, my grandfather came in from milking, his cheeks red from the cold. My grandmother and her daughters went out to the kitchen, and the men added leaves to the dining-room table. We sat down to eat, and Uncle Luther said grace. On the table, the dishes were piled high with boiled potatoes and carrots and string beans, boiled beef, and white bread. Everyone passed plates to and fro and talked all at once. My two aunts vied over me, teasing and praising.

"How was the hurricane up your way?" I heard my father say to Wash. He had to interrupt Wash to say it, but it was the only way you could ever ask Wash a question.

As I'm sure my father expected, it got Wash started. "I was coming back from chasing some bees—I found a hive, all right, but I needed a ladder—and I saw the sky looking mighty peculiar down over South Pasture way, and . . . " He told every motion he made and named every tree that fell on his land and the land of his neighbors. When he spoke about it, the hurricane took on a sort of malevolent personality, like someone cruel without reason.

The rest of the table talked hurricane, too. My grandfather told about a rowboat that somehow moved half a mile from its pond. My aunts talked about their towns, my father of how the tidal wave had wrecked his brother's island off the Connecticut coast. I told about walking home from school with a model airplane in my hand and how a gust of wind took it out of my hand and whirled it away and I never found it. (I didn't say that my father bought me another one the next day.) I had the sudden vision of all of us—the whole family, from Connecticut to New Hampshire—caught in the same storm. Suppose a huge wind had picked us up in its fists? . . . We might have met over Massachusetts.

After supper, we moved to the living room. In our family, the grown-ups had their presents on Christmas Eve and the children had Christmas morning all to themselves. (In 1938 I was the only child there was.) I was excited. The fire in the open stove burned hot, the draft ajar at the bottom and the flue open in the chimney. We heard the wind blowing outside in the darkness and saw white flakes of snow hurtle against the black windowpanes. We were warm.

I distributed the presents, reading the names on the tags and trying to keep them flowing evenly. Drifts of wrapping paper rose beside each chair, and on laps there were new Zane Grey books, toilet water, brown socks and work shirts, bars of soap, and bracelets and neckties. Sentences of package opening ("Now *what* could *this* be?") gave way to sentences of appreciation ("I certainly can use some handkerchiefs, Caroline!"). The bright packages were combed from the branches of the big tree, and the floor was bare underneath. My eyes kept moving toward a pile under and around the small tree.

"Do you remember the oranges, Katie?" said Uncle Luther.

My grandmother nodded. "Didn't they taste good!" she said. She giggled. "I can't think they taste like that anymore."

My grandfather said, "Christmas and town meeting, that's when we had them. The man came to town meeting and sold them there, too." He was talking to me. "They didn't have oranges much in those days," he said. "They were a great treat for the children at Christmas."

"Oranges and popcorn balls," said my grandmother.

"And clothes," said Uncle Luther. "Mittens and warm clothes."

My grandfather went out into the kitchen, and we heard him open the door. When he came back, he said, "It's snowing and blowing still. I reckon it's a blizzard, all right. It's starting to drift."

"It won't be like '88," Uncle Luther said. "It's too early in the year."

"What month was the blizzard of '88?" said my father.

Uncle Luther, my grandfather, and my grandmother all started to talk at once. Then my grandparents laughed and deferred to Uncle Luther. "March 11 to 14," he said. "I guess Nannie would have remembered, all right." My great-aunt

Nannie, who had died earlier that year, was a sister of Uncle Luther and my grandmother.

"Why?" said my father.

"She was teaching school, a little school back of Grafton, in the hills. She used to tell this story every time it started to snow, and we teased her for saying it so much. It snowed so hard and drifted so deep Nannie wouldn't let her scholars go home. All of them, and Nannie, too, had to spend the night. They ran out of wood for the stove, and she wouldn't let anyone go outside to get more wood—she was afraid he'd get lost in the snow and the dark—so they broke up three desks, the old-fashioned kind they used to have in those old schoolhouses. She said those boys really loved to break up those desks and see them burn. In the morning, some of the farmers came and got them out."

For a moment, everyone was quiet—I suppose, thinking of Nannie. Then my father—my young father, who is dead now—spoke up: "My father likes to tell about the blizzard of '88, too. They have a club down in Connecticut that meets once a year and swaps stories about it. He was a boy on the farm out in Hamden, and they drove the sleigh all the way into New Haven the next day. The whole country was nothing but snow. They never knew whether they were on a road or not. They went right across Lake Whitney, on top of fences and all. It took them eight hours to go the four miles."

"We just used to call it the big snow," said my grandmother. "Papa was down in Danbury for town meeting. Everybody was gone away from home overnight, because it was town meeting everyplace. Then in the morning he came back on a wild engine."

I looked at my grandfather.

"An engine that's loose—that's not pulling anything," he explained.

"It stopped to let him off right down there," my grandmother continued. She pointed through the parlor, toward the front door and across the road and past the chickens and sheep, to the railroad track a hundred yards away. "In back of the sheep barn. Just for him. We were excited about him riding the wild engine."

"My father had been to town meeting, too," said my grandfather. "He tried to walk home along the flats and the meadow, but he had to turn back. When it was done, my brothers and I walked to town on the tops of stone walls. You couldn't see the stones, but you could tell from how the snow lay." Suddenly I could see the three young men, my grandfather in the lead, single-filing through the snow, bundled up and their arms outstretched, balancing like tightrope walkers.

Washington spoke, and made it obvious that he had been listening. He had broken his monologue to hear. "I remember that snow," he said.

I settled down for the interminable story. It was late and I was sleepy. I knew that soon the grown-ups would notice me and pack me off to bed.

"I remember it because it was the worst day of my life," said Wash.

"What?" said my father. He only spoke in surprise. No one expected anything from Wash but harangues of process—how I moved the rock, how I shot the bear, how I snowshoed down Ragged.

"It was my father," said Wash. "He hated me." (Then I remembered, dimly, hearing that Wash's father was a cruel man. The world of cruel fathers was as far from me as the world of stepmothers who fed poisoned apples to stepdaughters.) "He hated me from the day I was born."

"He wasn't a good man, Wash," said my grandmother. She always understated everything, but this time I saw her eyes flick over at me, and I realized that she was afraid for me. Then

I looked around the room and saw that all eyes except Washington's were glancing at me.

"That Christmas, '87," Washington said, "the Kenestons' folks" (he meant my grandmother's family) "gave me skates. I'd never had any before. And they were the good, new, steel kind, not the old iron ones where you had to have an iron plate fixed to your shoe. There were screws on these, and you just clamped them to your shoes. I was fifteen years old."

"I remember," said Uncle Luther. "They were my skates, and then I broke my kneecap and I couldn't skate anymore. I can almost remember the name."

"Peck & Snider," said Wash. "They were Peck & Snider skates. I skated whenever I didn't have chores. That March tenth I skated for maybe I thought the last time that year, and I hung them on a nail over my bed in the loft when I got home. I was skating late, by the moon, after chores. My legs were good then. In the morning, I slept late—I was tired—and my father took my skates away because I was late for chores. That was the day it started to snow."

"What a terrible thing to do," said my grandfather.

"He took them out to the pond where I skated," said Wash, "and he made me watch. He cut a hole in the ice with his hatchet. It was snowing already. I begged him not to, but he dropped those Peck & Snider skates into the water, right down out of sight into Eagle Pond."

Uncle Luther shook his head. No one said anything. My father looked at the floor.

Washington was staring straight ahead, fifteen years old again and full of hatred. I could see his mouth moving inside the gray-brown beard. "We stayed inside for four days. Couldn't open a door for the snow. I always hated the snow. I had to keep looking at him."

After a minute when no one spoke, Aunt Caroline turned to

me and made silly guesses about the presents under my tree. I recognized diversionary tactics. Other voices took up separate conversations around the room. Then my mother leapt upon me, saying it was *two hours* past my bedtime, and in five minutes I was warming my feather bed, hearing the grown-up voices dim and far away like wind, like the wind and snow outside my window.

THE

FIFTY-DOLLAR

BILL

I am a lawyer in Akron, Ohio. I am respected in my profession and in my community. Among my associates respect is not accorded easily. I have never asked the judge who is my best friend to fix a traffic ticket for the son of my liquor dealer. I have never promised a favor to a detective in order to hide evidence unfavorable to my client. Many lawyers I meet in the courts have done these things and live on intimate terms with dishonesty. I call myself an honest man.

In 1942, just after Pearl Harbor, I was in my last year of law school and my wife was pregnant. We had seen the war coming and were married in June at the end of my second year. I had been deferred from the peacetime draft in order to finish school. I had no intention of avoiding service to my country and I expected, even before the Japanese attack, to go into the office of the judge advocate general in June, 1942.

The Japanese attack on December 7, 1941, changed everyone's plans. There was great confusion then about the draft, as anyone my age will remember. Some first- and second-year men quit law school to enlist, but we third-year students were determined to finish our degrees. For a while there were rumors, sometimes printed in the papers, that we would be drafted out of the classroom and into the infantry. For a while I must admit that I was anxious: In sight of my degree and my first child, I was to exchange my studies for basic training; after six and a half years of college and graduate school, I would be a private like the drugstore cowboys from high school. I had a dream at that time that surprised me, because it showed that I feared dying. It was not exactly a dream but a repeated sequence that I saw in my mind's eye even while I was awake, a film clip of my death. I was wading ashore from a landing craft, my rifle held over my head. Ahead of me was a small island of palm trees and tall grass. A shell exploded near me and shrapnel hit my legs. I was not badly hurt, but I could not stand up. I sank under the weight of my equipment, shouting for help that no one could give me, drowning in shallow green waters.

My father, who owned a department store in Canton, suggested that I write our congressman. Our family was prominent in politics and my name would be known as belonging to a good Republican family. Our representative redirected my letter to the army and the J.A.G.'s headquarters. I should say that I was interested in getting the J.A.G.'s office to request my deferment until graduation. Because my grades were good and I was an editor of the *Law Review*, I had something to say for myself.

Now I must go backward in time, because in January of 1942 I had forgotten something from the summer of 1941. That summer, after our marriage, I worked part-time in the law office of my wife's uncle. The rest of the time I was preparing the first issue of the *Law Review*, studying, and honeymooning. My wife wasn't working. Her uncle paid me a wage that was fair but insufficient and in order to get by we dipped into wedding-present money. My wife's grandfather had given us $500. Whenever we ran low that summer, we pulled out another of his fresh fifty-dollar bills. We hid the money under our bed, in the last envelope in a box of envelopes. When school started in the fall, Marion began to work as a university secretary, and we were able to live on her salary.

The J.A.G.'s office sent me a form letter that confused me and everyone to whom I showed it. I wrote to the man whose name was printed at the bottom, set forth my achievements, and said what I wanted. I drafted the letter a dozen times, typed it in a hurry, stuffed it into an envelope, and ran to catch the evening mail.

Four days later my father called from Canton, in such a rage that I could hardly understand him. I finally made out what he was saying, and understood what is obvious from the details of my story: I had enclosed my letter in the last envelope of the box under our bed, and the last fifty-dollar bill was still in it. To the man in Washington, my letter was an open, stupid, insulting attempt at bribery. He had called our congressman in a fury: Only personal regard for Congressman Morgan kept him from taking my letter to the FBI; the young man was not fit for the bar, much less the J.A.G.'s office. Whereupon Morgan called my father.

I convinced my father, finally, that it was merely an unfortunate coincidence. Of course I wrote letters to our representative—who died a year later, I suppose luckily for me—and the man at the J.A.G.'s office, but I never heard from them. If I had been they, I would never have believed this farfetched story. But the incident disturbed me deeply. I found that I had to tell the story over and over. In the navy—I was automatically deferred until graduation and found a commission without difficulty—I told everyone I met. Even after I came home and started practicing law in Akron, I told people. I suppose most of them believed me simply because I told them. Besides, as I emphasized earlier, I have a reputation for honesty. No one could believe I had been so corrupt or so stupid. Finally I grew tired of the story and stopped telling it.

But I did not forget it entirely. My son is twenty and a sophomore at the university. Last month he talked about transferring to the Air Force Academy if he could get in. He asked me to write our congressman. That night I had the most extraordinary dream. I was back in the apartment of our first year of marriage. Marion was wearing the brooch that she lost when I was in the Pacific; I saw myself in the mirror as I was at that time. Then I stooped under the bed to find an envelope for the letter I held in my hand. Then I licked the envelope and shut it, and saw, for a fraction of a second but clearly, a delicate line of green frothing upward against white paper like a sea made tiny but a sea in which I could drown.

WIDOWERS'

WOODS

Mr. Thomas swayed in the backseat of the taxi as it turned into the cemetery through the white wooden gate. The driver slowed down, nearly stopping; when he had checked his closeness to the gate outside his window, he pulled ahead into a gravel path. Mr. Thomas's vision behind his thick glasses was blurred, leaving only a tiny slip of clarity in the center. In the clear patch, he saw twin tire-tracks leading to the summerhouse. The cab charged up to it and braked, scattering cinders. Mr. Thomas heaved forward, bracing his hand against the seat cover to keep from falling. Charlie drove too fast. The lane was built for buggies.

The driver turned around and smiled at him. "Here y' are," he said.

"You drive too fast. There are too many cars on the roads," said Mr. Thomas.

"Here y' are," said the driver.

Mr. Thomas used his hands to help move his legs toward the door, which the driver leaned over to open for him. Mr. Thomas swiveled on the plastic cover and let his feet slide to the patchy cinders. When he felt steady, he leaned back inside the car and took out a long cylinder, full of green liquid, that ended in a sharp point. He propped the cylinder against the rail of the summerhouse and walked slowly around the taxi to the driver.

"Thank you, Charlie," he said. He took four quarters from his pocket and handed them to the driver.

"Name is Tony, Mr. Thomas. Charlie's dead. See you in an hour, right?" The driver smiled again. Mr. Thomas watched him go, from the keyhole of his sight.

It was hot. Mr. Thomas's mouth hung open. He walked into the green summerhouse and sat in the shade fixing his vision on the pump and the rusty watering can in front of him. Where should he start today? Last week, he had stopped at James Hartwell 1812–1884. Soon it would be Hettie again. He walked to the door. His fingers felt the roughness of the railing and when he looked he saw that the paint was peeling away. His vision played like the beam of a flashlight over the flaking paint of the wooden ceiling. Then he stepped through the door and saw that the outside paint was worse. Everywhere the wood was showing through, a dark brown fungus spreading over the summerhouse, reaching out its creepers. It was like October. The weeds turned brown and died, leaving bare patches of dirt when you raked the leaves. He remembered that he had mentioned the paint to the caretaker. Many times.

He picked up the green cylinder where it lay against the railing and walked into the graveyard. A breeze from the lake across the road came feeling through the heat. Mr. Thomas sensed beneath his shoes that part of the grass was cut and part was not. He straightened and swept his eyes in a circle until he saw the power mower, a bare-chested man behind it. The man waved and shouted, but Mr. Thomas did not hear him or the rasp of the mower. What was his name, the one who did not wear a shirt? Dino.

He passed the Hartwells and paused to read William Scrubbs and Mary His Wife. Moss made the dates hard to read. Mr. Thomas leaned on his green stick and rested. His vision moved to the street beyond the cemetery and the stores of glass and tile. He heard a noise and turned around. "Hi, Mr. Thomas," shouted the fat bare chest. "Dino. How you doing?" Dino smiled widely in his sweat.

"Crabgrass," said Mr. Thomas.

"You keep it in line," Dino shouted. "You got that thing." He pointed at the green stick. "That's a good thing."

"It's not enough," said Mr. Thomas. He began to feel despair again; Charlie would be back and he had not begun. He bent to the ground and found what he was looking for, the wide, scratchy, gray-green blades, spreading through the real grass that was frail and so easy to kill. He jabbed the point of his green cylinder into the center of the broad leaves and squeezed the bulb at the top.

"Well, so long, Mr. Thomas," said Dino, and rolled away, hitching his trousers over his stomach.

Mr. Thomas moved slowly, searching with the slot of his vision, finding the leaves, plunging and killing. Every minute he stood up and breathed slowly for a while, searching out a breeze to cool himself. Then he bent again and continued his work. The power mower came close to him, receded, and returned again. For a while he was absorbed. He smiled and a march tune went through his head. But there were so many. He was still at the Scrubbses'. He looked ahead. After them the Bullmers, and then Hettie's single stone.

Then he heard noises and there were children running through the cemetery, so many that they were like beetles scurrying in the grass. They had climbed over the fence in some war of blocks, and they were firing cap pistols at each other. He thought of the Fourth of July. His Uncle Harry's fife and drum corps, Victors of Vicksburg, had marched all day, full of cider. Boys threw firecrackers all day. Politicians talked, they denounced the Empires, the British Empire spreading all over the world. But then it stopped: An Italian threw a fire-cracker into an old lady's firecracker stand; she died, and the state passed a law forbidding fireworks. The children defend-ing the summerhouse, banging their guns, have black hair and dark faces. They spread everywhere like weeds.

Mr. Thomas left the Scrubbses' plot and walked past the Bullmers to Hettie's grave. He felt tired. Scanning Hettie's and his own grass, the swift shuttle of his vision revealed a crop of crabgrass larger than he had ever seen. Though a man fought it all his life, he could not win. It grew over everything; and when he stopped fighting it, it grew over him. He stabbed with his weed killer, jabbing so violently that he missed the roots he aimed for. Everywhere crabgrass spread its claws, the broad hated leaves. He swung at them with his stick, shouting at them, and tears rolled on his cheeks. Then he was so tired and hot that he had to lie down. Slowly and carefully he got down on his knees and his forearms, and then stretched out flat. Blades of crabgrass outlined his shape.

He opened his eyes to look into the heart of a weed: In the center of each plant, he saw a dark grove of trees; if he could get inside, there would be shade.

An old man in a farmhouse on the side of a hill in New Hamp-shire had been awake for hours. Ben had thought about the flavor checkerberry, about a baseball game between Andover and Wilmot in 1894, about his brother Willard who had died of influenza at the end of the war, and about holes in fences. He lay for a long time remembering a quarrel with his father, which ended with his father telling him stories about the family. Now the sun had risen over the shed, which meant, because it was September, that it was time to get up. What were his chores today?

He dressed quickly, long underwear and overalls and a brown shirt, thick brown socks and old black fancy shoes. In the kitchen the stove was cold; Ben struck a match and lit the oil ring that was set into the place where he had burned wood for fifty years. Slim pipes carried oil from a tank in the woodshed. The fire bloomed toward his hand; he set a kettle over the flame and spooned some Nescafé into a pink cup.

In the garden outside the kitchen window, which Nancy had tended herself, long-legged snapdragons angled toward the sun, horny flowers crumbled and brown with the frost of the night before last. On the lawn a rabbit skittered through tall grass; he thought of his gun; the sound of boiling turned him around. He drank the black coffee quickly and felt the heat uncoil down his arms and legs. He flexed fingers and toes: Time to be doing. What chores? He remembered going to bed tired and listing the chores for tomorrow.

When he was through with his cornflakes, he washed the empty dishes and left them to dry in the rack. The news. He turned on the radio and sat in a rocking chair under the empty canary cage, listening to news and weather. They pulled the boy out of that well. Flowered oilcloth covered the table in front of him; at the corners of the table the shiny surface had split and brown fibers showed through. He liked to rub his hand against the fibers. Above the table was a calendar, the month of August with a picture of field corn tall in the sun. He rocked back and forth. The weather was fair, Eastport to Block Island.

He put on a cloth cap and a suit coat and walked to the barn. Ghost cows turned to look at him as he walked in the empty tie-up. In a corner, where whitewash turned gray on spiderwebs, his three-legged milking stool hung next to his pail; for a few seconds he milked the herd and cooled the milk. He looked out the back window, where the necks of twenty horses had worn the sill smooth, at the dry bed of a stream, and at weeds turning gray with September frost.

On the main floor, old boards were still wispy with hay; clusters of harness hung from wooden pegs; ladders he had made himself led up to the first loft and from there to the second. He put his hand on the silky polished wood of a rung. Everything turned smoother, though he remembered slivers when the ladders were new. Birds flew in and out, over his head.

There were lumps of hay, nearly black now, under the eaves of the barn. Hay reminded him of a chore: He walked down the hill to the shed where he kept the hayrack and looked at the side with the missing spoke. In the woodshed he bent among ash sticks and picked one that he took back to the hayrack; he measured it against the gap; he drew a line on it with a pencil he found in his overalls. He was pleased to find it there. Then he sat on an overturned sap bucket and carved and smoothed the new spoke. His mind mumbled over stories, friends, smiling and shaking hands and eating fresh ice cream from a dish outdoors under a maple tree. When he was finished, he fitted the new spoke in place on the rack.

Back in the kitchen he hung up his cap and suit coat and lit the oil ring again. He rubbed his hands together above the flame and set the kettle over it. He opened the refrigerator and took out a plate of lunchmeat: Fourth day from that can. He sliced off a thick piece and put it on a clean plate, adding a handful of potato chips from a cellophane bag. Water boiled for his coffee; he sat at the set-tubs on a tall stool and ate lunch.

Then he washed and lay on the sofa in the sitting room where the air never moved. Because he had not yet started burning ash in the big square stove, he pulled a quilt over himself. For a minute he kept his eyes open, looking at the tall radio standing on its legs, at the glassed-in bookcase, stuffed with books and photographs, at the long table clock that never worked properly, and at the picture of Franconia Notch. What chore would occupy the afternoon? Then he slept lightly.

When he woke the sun shone into the parlor past the trailing ivy that Nancy had put in the window. He stood and looked out at the hayfields, big stone and mountain beyond. Hay waved, tall and gray-brown. Winter and snow would trample it down, and new grass would tangle with it next spring. A good hay day.

He clapped his hands together suddenly, making a noise like a rifle in the still room. He looked at the pictures on top of the piano and said out loud, "I'm going fencing." At least, he would take a look at the pasture fence. He was happy and he hummed a hymn tune, "I walked in the garden alone." It was a good day for walking in the pasture, sun and a light wind.

He put on his cap and jacket and walked up the road. Ahead of him was the big stone, a single boulder the size of a wood-shed, where—someone told him when he was a boy—the Indians had met for their powwows. As he went past it, he paused to touch the stone arrow in the side, a strange indentation shaped like an arrow, as clean and accurate as if it had been chiseled. He ran his forefinger from the point of the arrow around the whole shape of it, up the narrow stem, and into the wavy feather at the end.

He stepped through a gate in the fieldstone wall; the poles were out of their stone notches, lying on the ground. No need to set them back. He walked inside his wall as it turned a right angle and headed uphill. Then the wall turned into a fence of wire and felled branches, with holes where the wire had rusted through or a branch had rotted. He made a point of remembering the broken places.

As he walked more deeply into the old pasture, new pine grew tightly around him, and cowflops on the path next to the fence were gray and fragile with age. The pine made him think of coffins; but under his feet he felt the ridges of old ploughing. He had come to the potato place, as he had learned to call it when he was a boy, where his grandfather had cleared timber and planted potatoes, way back in the thirties before the Mexican War.

The fence disappeared entirely; pines grew smaller until they were gone. He climbed a rise and saw the bowl of a high valley before him, a smaller saucer of fertile land green with potato plants. At the far side three men and a boy were working, grabbing in clods with long-handled claws for potatoes. When they had dug up a hill they bent and gathered potatoes into the burlap sack each one carried with him. He walked across the harvested rows to join them. Anyone can use another hand. A man with a black beard leaned on his fork: "Will you give us a hand?"

He took over the tool that the boy had held. He dug a row of hills. Now the boy went row to row cropping potatoes into sacks. The men did not have to stoop and gather potatoes, and the rows moved faster. He dug easily and slowly in the loose soil, tossing aside the green plants with their brown, frostbitten edges. The muscles in his back grew tired, but he felt good. The sun lowered. A woman walked toward them along the edge of the field, coming from the direction of the farm. She carried a white enamel coffeepot and a wicker basket. They sat under a sugar maple and drank hot coffee, milk and sugar already mixed in it, and each ate a hard-boiled egg and a piece of custard pie. The bearded man and his son sat with the woman, apart from the two hands who ate steadily and silently. The bearded man asked him, "Will you stay to harvest?"

It was late; his back ached; he felt happily tired. "I'm going back," he said. "I'm obliged for the coffee and the pie."

He left them while they finished their coffee under the maple; he walked back the way he had come. A bear crashed past him in the underbrush, not seeing him. First time he'd seen a bear since he was a boy. The trees were huge and old; it was colder; he'd better light the stove in the sitting room. Though he was sure he was near it, he could not find the fence. When he came to the flat part, where the road was, he could not find the road. He felt his way in the direction of the house and came into a clearing where the big stone, as huge as a barn in the twilight, gathered the darkness of the forest. The side where he felt for the stone arrow was smooth.

Further, he found himself on a flat nook of land he recognized, but there was a grove of rock maple on it—great trees three hundred years old, trunks as hard as granite. He admired the broad, tough leaves, which were brilliant orange and red, and delicate yellow. He was lost, yet a comfortable laziness came over him. He stood on the matted leaves, in the middle of his sitting room, and after a while sat down and leaned back against a tree.

When Mr. Thomas found his way into the woods, the harsh light retreated; he felt cool and strong. He walked on matted leaves, not caring about the animals; he passed a huge boulder. Then he saw that the woods were full of old men, sleeping or sitting quietly by themselves. Widowers' Woods, he thought, that's what they ought to call it.

KEATS'S

BIRTHDAY

Richard's wristwatch chirred him awake at seven o'clock in the tall shadowy room on the Via Frattina near the Spanish Steps. He woke as usual feeling perky and swooped his hand along Eleanor's body under the comforter on this cool November morning; she stirred and murmured. In the dimness he picked out details of their room: washbasin, pale stained wallpaper, lavender brassiere, suitcases packed and ready, brightly wrapped packages from shops in the streets below. . . . He patted Eleanor's ribs until she murmured again, waking slowly, stretching luxuriously as a cat.

Tomorrow they would wake in their Rhode Island house, and in the afternoon Eleanor would see her surgeon for the six-month checkup. Anxiety fretted the corner of his mind; but there should be nothing to fear. Tomorrow also he would return to the store, to the aisles of paper clips, carbon paper, bond, staplers, and yellow pads. He would find how the stationery business had endured his absence. Doubtless tomorrow or the next day Eleanor would return to the notes for her dissertation on "Madeline's Chamber."

On the first of their ten days in Rome they had gone to the Protestant cemetery and the graves of Keats and Shelley. They paid homage to the dead poets and wandered near the pyramid of Cestius among monuments raised for English and American expatriates, with a few scattered Germans and Scandinavians. Eleanor make small cries of recognition discovering the literary dead: Constance Fenimore Woolson, Henry James's friend who had jumped from a window in Venice; Goethe's son, a sad story; and the famous unspeakable grief, famously spoken, carved into the tomb of Rosa Bathurst. For two hours they paced damp shaded alleys reading names carved on stone through ivy that straggled everywhere among hundreds of cats—all the stray cats of Rome gathered by the pyramid-tomb of Cestius, buried 12 B.C.: Cats crouched against marble, cats scooted from concealment, cats leapt from dark ivy.

That day when they returned to their room on the Via Frattina, they knew that their Roman holiday would be a good one. They napped, made love, walked by the Steps among rich and poor promenaders, and took dinner in a small restaurant where Eleanor's cries of pleasure continued, now over a plate of mussels.

This morning Eleanor rose on her elbow, found her glasses, and muttered that she didn't want to go. Her thick glasses made a disguise or carapace, he understood, together with the severe bun into which she coiled her long, graying hair; Eleanor's wild swooping abundant fall of hair, with her breasts and her rich mouth, made happy and humorous secrets of the private life. On this vacation late in October and early in November they patrolled in the Forum by day, visited Caracalla's baths, took in palazzi of the Renaissance, gasped at the enormity of the Vatican Museum—to return here every day to the secret life. When they visited the rooms four blocks away where Keats died, and Eleanor wept again over the other love in her life, they returned to this bed. Because her dissertation centered on "The Eve of St. Agnes," which Eleanor called the most erotic poem in the language, she asserted the continuousness of scholarship and private life. Richard had experimented with feeling jealous: But his rival was not only a scarce five-feet tall; he had been dead for a century and a half.

On Keats's birthday, which was Halloween, Eleanor bought violets from a vendor on the Steps and delivered them to the museum four flights up. It was late afternoon, early twilight, and when they descended to the gloomy piazza Eleanor proposed that they walk for a while before supper. After ten minutes of silence she began to talk. She spoke of Keats but Richard understood that other matters hid under her obsession. Among the quick, elegant promenaders her voice was low and steady. As they took early dinner at their favorite place, her throaty voice kept on. She told stories Richard had heard before but her urgency made them new: how Keats had thrown a wretched dinner out the window while Severn and the delivery boy watched; how he had kept Fanny Brawne's letters beside him, unopened, unable to bear the misery of reading her words when he knew he would never again see Miss Brawne who wore his ring; how when he died Severn cut locks of his damp hair.

After dinner they walked again in the hazy wet twilight of the Roman autumn. Eleanor spoke little: Richard saw tears on her cheeks. As they turned back toward the Steps, tired and gripping each other fiercely, they heard a sudden screech like a tomcat yowling: The door of a dim café burst open and three bodies hurtled out. Two young men were beating a third on the face and ribs. There were no more cries, only the sound of blows on flesh. Richard and Eleanor started backward. The victim fell to the sidewalk, his dark bleeding head tilted over the curb into the gutter, while the two assailants, puffing and rubbing their hands, swaggered back inside. Eleanor covered her mouth with her hand and retreated further. "Mama," said the young man. Richard started toward him, then stepped back. "Should I call someone?" he said nervously. "Should I get a policeman?" The young man rolled his head and opened his eyes. "Mama mia," he said. Then he stood up, lurching— a short, compact man in his midtwenties—felt his ribs and arms, blinked, and without speaking limped toward a black alley; they watched as he fell again, stood and staggered, reeling from side to side, into the narrow passage.

When they had caught their breaths, Eleanor pulled Richard by the elbow to peer down the alley. The young man was not to be seen. "I should have helped him," said Eleanor with abrupt bitterness. "I spend the day pitying someone who died a hundred and fifty years ago, but when a live boy bleeds in front of me I run away!" Her voice was vehement.

"What could you do?" said Richard. "It was all over before we could think. He's all right, he got up and walked away. You couldn't do anything."

Eleanor detached her arm. "You're the same," she said. "*'Should I call a policeman?'*" she mocked him. "Where were you when someone needed you?"

Richard's cheeks burned with instant humiliation and anger. *Why* would she suddenly claw at him? He had only tried to make her feel better! . . . Sullen resentment over injustice glowed in his cheeks as they walked back to the hotel rapidly and undressed without speaking. For a long time he could not sleep. When he heard Eleanor's even breathing he felt outrage and self-pity.

But in the morning they turned to each other and made up, without speaking of the night before, and as the day continued Richard felt his anger drain away and the old mild happiness return.

On this morning of their departure Richard took off his pajamas and stuffed them into a suitcase. He put on his traveling clothes, the same flannels and tweeds he wore at the store, and stowed their passports and airline tickets in the tweed jacket's inside pocket. "We'll come back," he said, "if not next year the year after."

It was not easy to leave the business; and his store manager was retiring. Eleanor's mother, recently widowed, stayed with Amos and Ada this time. Would it be easier or harder when they were teenagers? It had been four years since their last trip abroad, to London and Hampstead; it might be another four years before they could return.

"We'll come back," said Eleanor. "I'm sure we'll come back." She moved slowly, taking off her nightgown and packing it away. He looked at her: Forty years old, married fifteen years, she looked (he liked to tell her) as if she belonged on a calendar in a filling station. The scar on her left breast made only a pale line. Those great pillowy abundances—in public concealed under loose blouses and sweaters a size too large—thrust out, intact and luxurious, below the straight strong lines of her shoulders. How could *shoulders* be so sensuous? He gazed at her tiny waist under the faint swelling of stomach, the wild flag of pubic hair, the slim smooth columns of thigh and tapering leg. She turned away and his breath caught again at the sight of her buttocks. "*Eleanor*," he said.

She turned back to him, laughing, with a sound he heard only in private. "Not today," she said. "Tomorrow, back in our old bed, after the children quiet down . . ."

Ten days ago their charter landed, a cheap flight that lodged them at a monstrous suburban hotel fifty minutes from the Forum. They had migrated to their clean cheap *albergo*, and on this Sunday morning they would rejoin their group for the return flight. They would meet again the big-eyed man who was sure all Italians were gypsies; the woman who was always shortchanged; the honeymooners looking dazzled and solipsistic. . . .

This trip had been restitution for Eleanor and Richard. Only last April Eleanor, examining herself, had found a lump in her left breast: mammogram, biopsy, and the result from pathology—cancer, the unendurable word. Just a year earlier, she had held her father's hand as he died of it. . . . Now Richard and Eleanor clung to each other, cast away, as if they held to a board in mid-Atlantic; they wept and shuddered, dreamed and daydreamed their dread. For a week, while the medical universe consulted itself, they made no love. Then surgeon, pathologist, and oncologist sounded reassurance: The tumor was small, with no indication of metastasis; nothing suggested radical mastectomy, removal of lymph nodes, radiation, chemotherapy. A small incision removed the tumor. Gradually they stopped shaking, and cautiously their dreams turned benign: Eleanor withdrew from her teaching assignment this autumn as they made plans for the long-delayed journey to Rome.

This morning while he watched she stepped into a minuscule patch of silk underpant, bordello red, little strings with bows at each side. When Richard looked at Eleanor under pompous English Department circumstances—and her professors addressed him, the businessman, with hearty condescension, speaking of baseball, perhaps, or of new tax legislation—he smiled to think how underneath gray suit, straight skirt, and severe jacket, Eleanor blossomed at her skin with a hooker's underwear.

Dressed, packed, and ready this Sunday morning, they sat on the edge of their bed in the dingy light, early November and early morning, to eat the breakfast they had secreted the day before. (The usual café did not open on Sunday until ten o'-clock.) They sliced a mild cheese onto two rolls only slightly stale and finished with huge pears they had bought from a vendor at a crossroad.

Descending to the empty street, Richard carried two heavy suitcases while Eleanor arranged herself with camera, shopping bags, and briefcase. No one stirred on the Via Frattina and the brilliant shops were shuttered. Richard's eyes climbed to the peach and rose pastels, dirty and luxurious, of plastered upper stories. How Rome loved the body and the body's colors! He would remember this brightness in the pale beige of a Rhode Island winter: At every street corner, and sometimes midstreet, brackets overhead held pots of flowers—blooming in early November, shedding brightness over the crowded surge of handsome promenaders or in the silent empty morning blaring sensuous colors over Richard struggling with suitcases.

Surely they would find a taxi at the piazza. Walking, they swiveled their eyes in case the odd cab, cruising down a side street, might save them two hundred yards. Eleanor caught sight of one parked a block and a half away. Maybe it was waiting for someone, but it was worth a try; she trotted toward it leaving Richard to set down the suitcases and catch his breath. As she passed out of sight, Richard felt himself surrounded: Six small girls were suddenly jabbing and pushing at him like kittens at a mother cat. Each carried a square of cardboard and shoved it against him as if it were a plate for filling. Befuddled for a moment, Richard backed against a storefront. The skinny girls, quick as cats, were all black hair and dark eyes; then Richard thought: *gypsies!*

He shouted: "Get out! Scat! Get away from me!" His startled noises reverberated and disappeared in the empty street among the girls' urgencies. Then the girls skittered away down a side street as quickly as they had arrived. Eleanor hurried back without a taxi as Richard patted his rear pockets for the two wallets—dollars in one, credit cards in the other—that he had protected by pressing against the storefront. "Are you all right? Are you all right?" said Eleanor. "Were you shouting?"

Richard nodded. "Gypsies," he said. "Six girls." He pointed at them, gathered two blocks away and looking back in his direction. "They were all over me. . . ." Richard reached into the inside jacket pocket where he kept airtickets and passports: "They took our passports," he said.

He tried to think: Near the Spanish Steps they might find carabinieri. And what good would that do? By the time he brought a policeman back, the girls could have scattered to six different hiding places. The police would take him to the station; as their plane took off he would be telephoning the embassy to start replacing stolen passports. Meantime, the girls continued to loiter two blocks away. . . . Richard had a notion: "Please," he said to Eleanor, "stay with the suitcases."

He trotted toward the girls, looking around to see if there might be older brothers lurking; they waited as he approached. "I know you have our passports," he said in English with a calm that felt genuine; he had the thought: Why do I feel so calm? Why do I feel so competent? He said, "I will give you fifty dollars for the passports and tickets."

Six heads shook in outraged innocence. They spoke in Italian, but their bodies protested in formal or Victorian language, as he translated it later: "How can you possibly accuse us of such an enormity?" He looked into six nodding faces, so *sincere*; the eldest reminded him of Ada, nine years of solemn dark beauty. How *pretty* they were, black-eyed feline street-queens. . . . He pulled out his wallet, gripping it hard, and revealed the corner of a twenty.

Six twisting bodies edged closer. He backed against the wall again, wedging the credit-card buttock against it, and extended one foot waist-high while he revealed another twenty. Six sets of hands spread out, palms up: "Gracious sir, we are as poor as we are innocent." He showed another twenty.

Then the smallest of the girls reached a hand into her trouser-front and pulled out tickets and passports together. She approached him holding them out, her head cast down in demonstration of admitted guilt. Immediately the five larger girls crooned a chorus of *shame* at the youngest, each wiping one finger over another in a gesture Richard remembered from the playgrounds of childhood: "Shame! Shame! Shame! How could you embarrass us so? . . . but *because* you have embarrassed us so, we graciously consent to share in your reward." Twelve hands grasped for dollars. Richard distributed three twenties, gripped passports and tickets securely, and trotted back to Eleanor.

When they leaned into the backseat of their taxi, driving at great speed over empty roads to the airport, he repeated details of his story, recognizing excitement and even pleasure in the telling. As his heartbeat slowed down he patted Eleanor's shoulder; he could not stop smiling. Then he noticed that Eleanor, who at first shared his excitement, looked pale and stared straight ahead while he chattered. "Is something wrong?" he said.

She shook her head and forced a smile. "No," she said. "I suppose . . . Why weren't you angry with them? They were *robbing* us."

Richard felt a quick, familiar collapse of mood. Of course Eleanor was right. There was something lacking in him. He was not John Keats: He was ordinary, complacent, mild, and agreeable. Too mild: If it had been Richard, coughing to death in the Piazza de Spagna, he would not have thrown the bad dinner out the window, he would have eaten it, he would even have praised it, to please the delivery boy. And he would have read Miss Brawne's letters, and wept as he answered them. He would have apologized for dying. . . . Richard felt foolish, remembering the night of Keats's birthday when Eleanor was angry.

He fell silent; he watched the quickly lapsing ruined landscape of industrial Italy as roadsigns steered them toward the airport. Gradually his mind again rehearsed details of the morning's story; he felt his mood lift or lighten. Really, things were all right. . . . They would fly safely home to house, children, bed, and tomorrow's checkup. If nothing else, the gypsy girls had given him a story to tell, a mild adventure with a happy ending. Of course it was hardly an *ending*, but it was happy enough and it would do. As Eleanor leaned against him again, she squeezed his arm in clear affection and glanced up with a private look that registered anticipation: yes, not today but tomorrow . . .

MR.

SCHWARTZ

Carter Goldberg was a tutor in Lowell House at Harvard, while he finished his Ph.D. in Fine Arts. Although his area of study was ninth-century Byzantium, he indulged himself in a taste for ready-mades. In his window, which overlooked the larger of the two quadrangles, he hung what he called his Sacred Found Objects. One day it was a shiny intact Volkswagen tail pipe. A week later it was a four-foot-wide set of false teeth. By this time (he had lived in the house three years) most of his Sacred Found Objects were gifts from the boys. He was the most popular of the young tutors, especially with young men who had prepared for the college at the schools nicknamed St. Grottlesex. In the dining hall they paused at the end of the cafeteria line, their round trays crowded with meat loaf and glasses of milk, searching with sleepy eyes for Carter's table. To win his favor, they brought him Sacred Found Objects.

To Carter, the boys were themselves Objects—pleasant, articulate, gracious Objects. If he was a bit of a snob, he was certainly aware of it. When at seventeen he had taken a scholarship to Williams, instead of a slightly better one to Columbia, he had understood his social motives. But he was not anti-Semitic. His best student was a Brooklyn boy, also named Goldberg, *very* Jewish, and Carter admired him, helped him, invited him to parties with his Objects, and even liked him. No, he assured himself, his snobbery was not debilitating. Carter was twenty-five.

Chiefest of all the Objects was a boy from St. Paul's called Humphrey Bigelow, nephew of the Humphrey Bigelow who had been ambassador to the Court of St. James. He was chiefest because he combined the qualities Carter admired: intelligence, taste, money, and patrician good looks. Like most of Carter's clique, Humphrey did not major in Fine Arts. Most took History or Economics, and half of them intended to enter the foreign service upon graduation. Humphrey, on the other hand, was thinking of becoming an Episcopal priest, and majored in philosophy because it tested his theology.

Carter twitted him about his religion, as he twitted all his Objects. When they were pompous or argued stupidly, his irony reduced them to humiliated giggles. And when they were depressed, Carter stayed up all night with them, talking with intelligent sympathy, and they neither ran away to become migrant laborers nor threw themselves into the Charles from the boathouse dock. In return, they invited Carter to their parties and to lunch with their mothers at Chez Joseph's.

Then Humphrey Bigelow took Carter for a weekend to his people's place on Stayre Island off Long Island Sound in Connecticut. It was the May before Humphrey graduated. (He would go to England in the autumn, to Cambridge on the Lionel de Jersey.) They arrived Friday at dinnertime and Carter was delighted that Humphrey's Uncle Humphrey was also there. The whole island was Bigelows and people married to

Bigelows. The buildings were mostly old, heavily built summer cottages, with one or two modern houses wedged decoratively among high rocks. Everything Carter saw was good: the rugs, the furniture, the two or three paintings. He examined, judged, put into categories: there were few *gems*—a Cézanne drawing, certainly the exquisite Gonzales figure of a standing woman—but there was a decorum that was better than gems.

Humphrey Bigelow the elder took to Carter immediately. He overheard him teasing his nephew with a light irony, and he laughed for a long time and looked at Carter the way so many of the undergraduates looked: What exotic plant have I discovered? After dinner, when everyone made himself a Scotch and picked someone to talk with, Carter found himself chosen by the ambassador, who took him off to the small library and sat him down. Bigelow was about sixty-five, Carter decided, and vain about his looks: tanned, athletic, short gray hair, vertical creases in his cheeks, a curious youthfulness that was almost childish. Bigelow pulled a book from the shelf, E. E. Cummings's *Is V*.

"I was reading this man only last week," said Bigelow. Carter understood that Bigelow considered Cummings avant-garde. "Wonderful poet."

"I don't like him," said Carter. When Carter said something like this to an older man, he smiled charmingly to remove anything insulting from the contradiction. Older men enjoyed being engaged by the young, he realized, if the attack was not insulting; it made them feel younger.

"Why not?" said Bigelow.

"He makes up emotions out of books. 'All in green went my love riding.' Pseudo-Elizabethan. He's all right when he's hating things, like "Poem, or Beauty Hurts Mister Vinal," but he's bad at love. He doesn't understand anything about love."

They talked for three hours. At first, Carter listened and

nodded. It came to seem more and more that this Humphrey Bigelow was really the other Humphrey Bigelow. In the older man's eyes, Carter read the same nervous candor, the fear, the movement toward what young Humphrey called "goodness," and the countermovement that cherished family and wealth. Carter began to interject himself into the conversation, as he did with his undergraduates, mocking flagrant self-pity or exposing illogic, then murmuring in sympathy when he was moved to. When Bigelow found himself corrected, he looked admiringly at Carter.

After several scotches, Bigelow began a long, connected story of family scandal that included a dead grandfather's dead mistress, a missing will, and other properties of melodrama. Carter heard stories that would once have divorced husbands and disinherited nieces. One of the elder Bigelows present was quite possibly not a Bigelow at all, since his mother had been having an affair with a New York broker named Van Grierson the year before his birth. Carter felt disturbed by this last suggestion, as if a favorite mosaic were proved a forgery.

Yet Carter was flattered, if a bit puzzled, to be taken into Bigelow's confidence. He was flattered again the next morning when Bigelow picked him up for tennis, and beat him, and then told him more stories to go with their lobster salad at the ambassador's modern house high on a rock cliff. At teatime Carter was released and returned to his hosts for the last twenty-four hours of his weekend. Late Sunday afternoon, when Carter and Humphrey left Stayre Island, Uncle Humphrey waved good-bye from the dock.

In July Carter saw Bigelow again. Young Humphrey was in Greece, touring before he went up to Emmanuel. (In August arrived a pink plastic reproduction of the Venus de Milo, "Authentically Purchased on the Slopes of the Parthenon," which Carter hung in his Lowell House window.) Carter was concentrating on his dissertation, working late at the Fogg because it was summer and his social life had dwindled. One morning, walking between Houghton Library and the President's house, he saw Humphrey Bigelow the elder coming toward him. Bigelow was smiling, but Carter could read in his face that the recognition was incomplete. Bigelow was trying to place him, much as Carter would try to place, according to period and artist, a fragment from Byzantium. When they were a few feet apart Bigelow's hand went to his hat and he greeted Carter, and in a moment—Carter's useful irony protecting him, making him quickly invulnerable—he understood why Bigelow had felt able to confide in him.

"Good morning," Humphrey Bigelow said with confidence, "Mr. Schwartz."

THE FIGURE

OF THE WOODS

The Bunting farm is still there, more intact than most of the countryside. In most of this portion of western Massachusetts, the farmland died long since and disintegrated into stony earth. Or city people bought the old farms and fixed them up and kept them on view like Lenin.

Thirty years before, when Alexander Bunting spent wartime summers there, three other farms had worked the fields between this house and the post office–store a mile away. Now there were none. The Bargers' big house had rotted away; the Luce place shone with aluminum siding, a trailer parked in the barnyard; the Whippelses' belonged to people from Cambridge now. Only the Bunting place still looked the same, or as near as it could without cornfields and cattle. Alexander's grandfather Luke died just after the war. His grandmother, a widow for twenty-odd years, had kept the farm tidy and the roofs shingled, but as she grew into her eighties, then celebrated her ninetieth birthday, she had given up her sheep, her chickens, and her vegetable garden. Her knees were too stiff. And now, at ninety-five, she could take care of herself no longer. Speechless, vague, incontinent, old Sarah lay in a bed all day in the home at Hubert's Falls, opening her mouth to the nurses' spoons at feeding time.

One Friday in July, Alexander Bunting, just divorced, picked up his son in Lincoln and drove west to open the musty farmhouse for a weekend. Davis was nine years old, small, and so astigmatic that his heavy glasses seemed to pull his frail head forward. Alexander wanted to *give* him the farm, or at any rate the feeling-farm, and had been frustrated on earlier visits with his wife, Elizabeth—Elizabeth annoyed at the Sears plumbing, at lumpy beds and calendar kittens, at drinking water with specks in it—who seemed to want to protect Davis, as if the farm carried germs that might infect him.

On the trip west, smooth in the old Porsche, Alexander had inquired discreetly into Davis's preferences. Davis's eyesight kept him from taking pleasure in games of catch. He liked to read and had brought with him a stack of Agatha Christies, but Davis could read anywhere—Alexander was careful not to speak this aloud—and now they were in the country. Alexander wanted to make his son a present of the past, but a father is not a grandfather, and he felt frustrated: Alexander Bunting who works for John Hancock in Boston is not Luke Bunting, wiry from chopping wood all his life, who loved walking all over his mountain on the pretext of fixing fences, and who talked constantly to his grandson, telling him stories of the old days when the little towns of western Massachusetts, two miles apart and each with its own depot, thrived with an energy that astonished young Alexander.

Davis listened politely, seat-belted alongside his father, while Alexander listed the opportunities of the farm: swimming, and they could get face-masks and flippers maybe; hiking, and he could show the cellar-hole of the house his great-great-grandfather had brought his bride to; fishing . . . when he started to speak of fishing, Davis interrupted him: Yes, he wanted to go fishing; *that's* what he wanted to do.

And although Alexander wondered if Davis had not merely picked one item from the list, perhaps the item that seemed least strenuous, still he was pleased. Alexander grew quiet as he drove, and daydreamed back to fishing. He remembered trout fishing the Ben Watts Brook when he was fourteen or fifteen. He remembered earlier catching pickerel from a row-boat in the pond. Earlier still, he remembered a day when he and Luke—Alexander couldn't have been more than ten—had walked a mile and a half, past a corner of the pond, to turn over some hay that had been rained on. Walking back with their pitchforks, over the little wooden bridge where Black Pond became Cold River, suckers poised fat and still in the water under the bridge. Like a boy, Luke couldn't resist. "Watch this, Alex," he said, and he hurled his pitchfork like a harpoon and speared a sucker. Retrieving fork and fish was difficult—but the cats in the barn had a feast that night.

When they reached New Harbor, Alexander parked at the sporting goods store and bought two rod-and-reel sets shrink-wrapped in tough plastic. Then they drove on ten miles, and turned in to the driveway just as dusk filled up the hollows between house and barn. Alexander stared at the farmhouse a moment before unpacking the small trunk and going inside. The place seemed still faintly alive, like his grandmother prostrate in the gray room at Hubert's Falls. He would go and see her, this trip, even if she didn't know him. Davis should see his great-grandmother one more time before he saw her in her coffin.

The electricity was off. Davis edged closer to his father as

Alexander flipped the switch repeatedly. Alexander felt panic start in his alien son. Then he realized it was his own panic he felt. Don't let everything go wrong. He remembered that over the sink there was always an oil lamp next to the kitchen matches. In rural Massachusetts electricity was luxurious and inconstant, like the dancing girl in the gold-mining town. He struck a match, lit the lamp, and led Davis into the shadowy living room. Snapshots of uncles and cats, in Woolworth frames, sparkled on tables and threw hovering patches of gloom on the walls. Beyond it were two bedrooms next to each other, with a common door.

The earlier you fish in the morning the better, as he remembered. Alexander waked at seven and tiptoed to look into Davis's room. Davis was reading a Miss Marple. The electricity had returned and yellow light circled Davis, haloing his tender skull. "Let's go fishing," said Alexander.

"Sure," said Davis. "I'm hungry."

Alexander had planned to return for breakfast later, or, more likely, to drive from the pond to the motel snack bar four miles away and eat a big hot breakfast together, father and son; pancakes and bacon and blueberry muffins.

"OK," he said. "Let's see what we've got." In a bag in the car were bread and jam. In the pantry there was an unopened jar of peanut butter. He found the toaster and toasted some bread and they ate peanut butter and jelly sandwiches for breakfast. Davis kept reading, explaining that he was at a good part. Alexander alternated between excitement and discouragement. When he looked uphill to the barn, or down at the narrow boards of the kitchen, or at the frayed oilcloth covering the set-tubs, he felt a surge of excitement. He knew it was a cliché but this farm seemed more *real* than Boston and work. Boston and work were intangible, abstract, a conspiracy-to-be-real designed by a gang of adults. This kitchen was uncontrived, accumulated over decades by decisions out of the Sears catalogue. Yet when he looked at Davis, whose thick glasses peered into a paperback book, he was separated again from set-tubs and floor. How could he marry his son to the old world?

While spreading the bread, he had explained to Davis the procedures observed for fishing. First, there was bait. When they had swept up their crumbs—no use encouraging the army of mice—and torn their rods out of the plastic casing, they found a shovel in the barn and proceeded to dig for worms. Alexander remembered digging for worms with his grandfather in a patch of hollyhocks beside the barn next to the beehives. He remembered skirting the beehives cautiously when he dug worms thirty years ago. During the war years, when frequent trains carried tanks and guns past the farm, and cars were rare, they had fished in the pale yellow twilight of July and August after milking and returned with pickerel and horned pout for his grandmother's kitchen and wormy perch for the village of cats.

Alexander sank the shovel into the loose dirt and turned it over. The black clump wriggled with pink tentacles. Davis took half a step back. Beside them as he dug, like a row of shanties in an abandoned town, wooden beehives crumbled in disrepair. Even the bees had deserted; but not the worms. Alexander filled a mason jar with earthworms and handed it to Davis, who carried it gingerly but without complaint as they walked to Black Pond. They crossed the railroad tracks—one train a day now—behind the foundations of the sheep barn. In the old fishing, Alexander and his grandfather had used the rowboat, always tied at the edge of the pond, and rowed over the silent, buggy water to secret good places. Without a rowboat, Alexander steered them to the narrow end of the pond, where it turned into the Cold River, to the bridge where he remembered his grandfather harpooning the sucker. Suckers weren't trout or pickerel, in the way of eating, but Davis wouldn't mind. He didn't eat fish anyway.

They found no fish at all except minnows. For half an hour they stood on the bridge and cast their lines to one side or the other, interrupted only by early-morning delivery trucks crashing up the dirt road to take newspapers and bread to the summer people or the boys' camp on the other side of the pond. After half an hour, a crisp, recorded reveille burst from loudspeakers at the camp. Alexander remembered how superior he had felt, as a boy, to the regimented squads from the camp, hiking past the farm when he had lived to his own tune. Davis was going to camp in July; all the boys at his school were going.

"Let's try somewhere else," said Davis. "Is there another place?" Alexander was pleased with Davis's perseverance. They walked north around the pond, through an uncut hayfield that grew between the railroad and a rim of birch and pine surrounding the pond at water's edge. The field narrowed and turned scrappy. Brush grew in a narrow space between trees and tracks, and they walked single file. Then the space widened and dipped into marshy grass. As they cut down toward the shore, they heard the daily freight rattle behind them heading for Springfield.

It was here that Alexander had walked with Luke to unfasten the rowboat and slide off into the still twilight, after bailing the water that had rained or leaked into the little boat, in stillness broken only by the sound of their oars slipping in the flat lake. Usually they had been alone on the pond; sometimes in midsummer a counselor from the camp would be fishing in a far corner in one of the camp's green rowboats; sometimes at the far end near the Cold River they could make out Charlie Buzzard's boat, with Charlie puffing his pipe into the soft increasing darkness. Charlie was postmaster-storekeeper two miles south on Route 40. Charlie's legs were bad and he brought his crutches into the boat with him; Alexander remembered that as a boy he had decided that crutches were like life preservers on land, which was not exactly so.

And Alexander now, with his young son beside him, walking slowly through scratchy bushes, remembered next his old fear of the pond. The farm women were afraid of water. He remembered his grandmother clucking like a hen about the pond; he remembered Great-Aunt Bertha whose fear was pathological: Women never learned to swim in the old days. He had been warned so often, so heavily—even though he was a good swimmer, taught at the Y in Brookline—that he had learned to fear the lake with a delicate, pleasant, almost erotic fear. There was a drowned man in the water. Years before, a summer worker at the boys' camp, an Irishman from Boston, had drowned one night swimming after work, and his body had never been found. When Alexander ran to the pond's edge as a little boy—first to get to the shore—he looked for the body washed up on the sand. When he fished, he expected to catch his hook on the drowned man and haul a skeleton out of the water.

Alexander and Davis moved close to the water. Their feet pushed little graves into spongy grass. They found a dry, sandy patch to stand on and untangled their lines. Water lilies lay thick on the water to the right of them, but straight ahead the pond was dark and clear. Alexander cast Davis's line as far as he could and handed the pole to Davis. Almost immediately the cork bobbed with a nibble; Davis jerked on his pole; the cork grew still, small nibbler frightened away. Davis turned and looked at Alexander. "Let's reel it in," said Alexander, "and see if he got the worm." Davis reeled in but when the cork was nearly to shore the hook snagged on something. Davis pulled but the line tautened and the pole bent. The hook was caught near shore, to their right near marshland and lily pads. Alexander told Davis to lay down his pole, and the two of them edged cautiously toward the hook. Their feet sank; muck seeped in their shoes. Davis made a little whimpering sound and held back. Feeling irritated, Alexander kept on.

The hook was caught on a piece of wood, a long curved edge of old timber at the edge of the water, narrowly rising edgewise from the sand. He tried the wood with his foot to see if it would bear weight. Then he realized that the wood was the side of a sunken rowboat and at the same time he knew it was Luke's; this was the place, the exact place, where his grandfather had kept the boat.

Alexander leaned down and scraped at the sand, excavating a moment of prow. Seeing him dig, Davis edged forward until his feet met the firmer sand near the boat, then knelt and dug also while Alexander told him what they had found. They scraped away enough sand to uncover the iron ring, a bit of rotten rope still tied to it, that had held it to shore. If they had dug further, Alexander was sure, they would have found the lace-rust skeleton of the coffee can that he had bailed with.

Now he loosened the hook and returned with Davis to fishing. They walked back to the farm half an hour later. Small perch had eaten their worms, and they had caught nothing to feed to the furred ghosts that crept in the barn.

That afternoon Alexander steered them away from fishing. Instead, they rode and walked over dirt roads. Alexander showed Davis grown-up fields where he had hayed with his grandfather, cellar-holes of farms that had supported generations of farm families, and old houses he had visited thirty years before. On a Sunday afternoon Luke would back the horse into the buggy, harness him—the only work done on a Sunday; dinner was cooked the day before and warmed up—and they would pay a social call on a neighbor a mile or two away, usually someone too old to get out, a frail lady, bundled in August, whom Sarah had known in school, or a blind man

Luke had played baseball with. Now the old houses were sometimes empty and tottering, blackened with rain and neglect, moving toward collapse; or sometimes a huge family squatted in them and looked suspiciously out at Alexander's slowing car as he pointed to a porch sagging among junked cars and old mattresses.

After an hour of loops and crisscrosses on back roads, Alexander turned the car onto the highway. Time for visiting hours at the old folks' home in Hubert's Falls. He reminded Davis that his great-grandmother was very old now; Davis said he remembered. Alexander said that she didn't stand up anymore, that nurses fed her, she didn't wear her teeth anymore, and she almost never spoke. Davis nodded solemnly.

The nursing home was old and wooden, the sort of old folks' home, Alexander thought, that makes headlines: 27 DIE IN REST HOME HOLOCAUST. Inside, no one seemed to be in charge. Old women in bathrobes—and one old man—sat in a parlor and gaped in the direction of a television set. In an alcove one group of visitors chatted quietly with a woman in a wheelchair. There were flowers everywhere but the rooms gave off only the odor of hospital—antiseptic and starch and chemical deodorizer, and underneath everything the smell of urine. Then a fat middle-aged woman in white entered the parlor with a pile of newspapers and dropped it on a footstool. None of the old people seemed to notice. Alexander stopped her as she turned to leave. "Please," he said. "We've come to see Sarah Bunting. My grandmother."

"Upstairs, that corner," she pointed. "Last one. She's doing real good. Pretty as a picture."

Alexander took Davis's hand and they mounted the stairs and found the room. Sarah was lying propped up in bed with her eyes wide open. She's dead, he thought with sudden horror, and then he saw an eyelid flicker. Alexander smiled falsely and spoke in a loud voice, introducing himself and Davis. Sarah looked straight ahead and blinked. The room was tiny and bare. Closet, chest of drawers with birthday cards—four months old—arranged on top, bedside table with medicine, window looking out on parking lot and general store. "We drove up yesterday," shouted Alexander. Davis looked at his bellowing father curiously. "Davis and I went fishing this morning. . . . Didn't catch anything . . . Heh-heh."

Against the gray pillow his grandmother's face sank slowly back into its bones. A fleshy woman in middle age when he first remembered her, the flesh had begun to leave her when she was eighty-five. At her ninetieth birthday, vain, lively and attractive, she had looked almost stylish in her black dress and her Newberry's pearls. Now the skeleton showed through, fine old bones under gray wax skin. Bony shoulders stuck out of a blue nightgown and her small arms lay straight at her sides, veined and raw-looking, ending in the big working hands and large knuckles, still bearing the wedding ring that she had worn for seventy-five years. Her blue eyes, large and miraculous, stared up at him. Maybe she was trying to puzzle him out.

Blue eyes moved and Sarah was staring at Davis. Davis looked back, then fidgeted and turned to look out the window. This must be unpleasant for him, Alexander thought; it's time to go. He began to address Sarah in the special voice, but he noticed her lips jerking in an effort of speech. Looking at Davis, she made a tentative noise, "Alex? . . . Alex? . . . " and Alexander knew that the old brain had found a resemblance. "That's *Davis*," Alexander said. "*I'm* Alex. That's *Davis*." Her lips sagged back into quiet and her stare turned vacant again. "Well," said Alexander, "I reckon it's time we left. Supper time," he said, and, suddenly with tears, knowing she would not understand but wanting to move closer to this wax body, "It's milking time," he said. "Time to go to the tie-up."

He pulled Davis after him and went downstairs to the car, and they drove to the farm in silence.

Davis was early to bed, taking his book. Alexander sat up and drank Scotch. Saturday night. He began to feel sad, a comforting sadness because it was a sadness that watched itself being sad and pitied itself. The Scotch was ten thousand tiny mirrors. He *could* not feel close to Davis. Davis was a city child, Elizabeth's child. Which was understandable, of course. But Davis could not seem to accept, even to comprehend—for all his IQ, which his mother mentioned from time to time—this old farm world that Alexander wanted to give him. Davis was polite, of course: Davis looked; Davis said, "I see," but Davis walked always inside a clear strong shell, like his glasses but thicker, a shell—Alexander thought, as the Scotch warmed him past self-pity into mental energy—made of Country Day and poodles named Harold Bloom and piano lessons and Recommended Reading at the Carnegie Library.

Tomorrow they would *fish!* His brain raced and he felt optimistic. They mustn't go back to the pond, which was as empty as the barn. There was no dark life hidden there any more—only the skeleton of a boat—and no slim pickerel slipping handsomely through weeds and black water. Again he remembered the Ben Watts Brook, the trout stream north of the pond, a tributary. His grandfather had taken him to it; they had fished it early one morning and returned with two trout that Sarah cooked for breakfast. Suddenly he felt a rush of enthusiasm, optimism. He knew he was drunk, but as always when he was drunk he knew it didn't matter.

Now he was able to remember the visit to Sarah, this afternoon. He laid it out in front of him, as if it were a map he were spreading on a table. The Scotch made it possible for him to think and at the same time to direct his thinking. Well, it was not one of those ghastly homes you read about, where senile people were abused and neglected. You could tell that. And after all, she was ninety-five years old. A full life. Then Alexander heard his cliché and laughed out loud at himself.

He looked at the room he sat in. How many years since

someone had had a drink here? Or was it the first time ever? His grandmother's temperance pledge, signed when she was twelve and adhered to without temptation for eighty-three years, hung over the bed he would sleep in. In this room old oval photographs hung on the walls—Luke, Sarah, Alexander's dead mother when she was small, Alexander's dead Uncle, his dead Great-Uncles and -Aunts, his three living second-cousins—and all the cats and dogs. He felt a rush of tenderness throughout his body. When his grandmother died, the farm would be left among five people—himself, his cousins, and Davis. The cousins would want to sell it and divide the money. No! He would buy it; it must not leave the family. He could come weekends from Boston with Davis to go fishing. He could come Christmas, summer vacation; maybe he could take leave from the firm and spend an autumn here some day. No, he thought with sudden strength and conviction, he would leave the firm, leave business forever, and live on the farm himself. He would grow vegetables, keep some chickens, shoot a deer every autumn.

Gradually he drifted into his boyhood dream of surviving as a self-sufficient farmer, the solitary Swiss Family Robinson of this country hill. He slipped quietly into this old dream and saw himself in a series of pictures: He is writing a book, as he always wanted to; he is feeding the hens; he saddles his horse; he catches a line of pickerel; he salts down fish; he cans tomatoes; his hens lay eggs, which he stores in water glass; he stalks a rabbit in the woods; he sets traps for muskrat and badger; he milks his cow in the twilight.

He slid rapidly and pleasantly through his dream as if he skied gently downhill. Feeling a slight discomfort in his face, he realized that he was smiling from ear to ear. Then he understood that his happiness was only the Scotch and he decided to go to bed. Just as he was turning out the light, he felt convinced that the house was crowded with family dead who disapproved of him: of his divorce, of the silly life he led, of his drunkenness, of his vain dreams. But he summoned irony to help him, and he laughed at himself out loud, and he soon slept.

Sunday morning, and the last day at the farm. Tonight they would drive silently east among all the other returning weekenders, back to Lincoln and Boston. Tomorrow he would go back to work on the new group life contract with Sol Reitman, sitting at the green desk all day. Alexander had wakened with a dry mouth and regrets; he must stop drinking alone. He remembered with disgust his daydreams of living on the farm. What was he supposed to do for alimony? For tuition? But then he remembered his plan for fishing the Ben Watts Brook— and he told Davis, who seemed enthusiastic.

But as they finished their peanut butter and jelly sandwiches, the sky darkened and the undersides of the maple leaves turned up in gusts. Then the wind blew harder and the air turned solid with dark water; wind took leaves from the maple and stuck them to the white clapboards of the house; the lights flickered and went out; the telephone made strange noises; lightning surrounded the house and seemed to walk through it. Davis made a frightened noise and moved closer to Alexander, which allowed Alexander to feel a tenderness for his son that he wanted but seldom felt.

The wind died down and the rain steadied itself, but it was too wet for fishing and the water too churned up. Alexander lit a candle and dug out the dominoes he and his grandfather had played with, old and smooth as felt, round at the corners. In an hour the lights came back, and soon after the rain stopped entirely. Sun steamed rain off leaves. Alexander took Davis on a tour of the barn. Then they drove four miles to the motel snack bar and ate cheeseburgers for lunch. The heat turned drier; Alexander wondered if they might be able to fish after all. The sensible thing would be to leave the farm after lunch, reach Boston at a reasonable time, and get a good night's sleep—but then they would have had only their one unsatisfactory experience of fishing, which might sour Davis on it forever.

Alexander realized that, for whatever reason, he was determined to fish the Ben Watts Brook.

After lunch they packed up and loaded the little car. Then they dug worms again. Alexander didn't mention that worms were supposed to be unacceptable to trout; it would have been a long drive for flies; and really, he liked digging for worms if only because it proved that something still lived on the farm.

He thought he remembered how to get to the Ben Watts Brook. Luke had driven the buggy there, quite a distance north of the farm, but Alexander gradually realized that he was past the turnoff. He felt frustration mounting. Seeing a dirt road that led in the right direction, he abruptly turned off the highway. They could give it a try. His head pounded, partly hangover and partly excitement. They drove past a tar paper shack next to a trailer and a patch of early corn. At a fork, he chose the left with no reason. The road began to peter out; the town seemed to be letting it go; branches scraped the side of the car and the surface of the road bumped like a riverbed. To the right Alexander saw a flat place where he could turn around and swung in slowly. Davis peered intently over the dashboard.

As he turned in, Alexander noticed two things at once; they were turning in to the driveway of a once-elegant farmhouse, unpainted but still upright; and just ahead the road led to a rickety bridge with water rushing underneath it. This *had* to be the Ben Watts Brook upstream. With satisfaction Alexander turned off the ignition and the sound of moving water, fast because of the big rain, filled the small car.

"Here?" said Davis.

"Here," said Alexander. "This is the place." From the back-seat he took fishing rods and worms and an old sap bucket—to keep the trout in—and set them down in the road. He had never seen the house before, and he couldn't take his eyes off it. He walked toward it, Davis following him hesitantly.

It was Greek revival, barely articulated pillars beside the doors still flecked with white paint, a pretty fanlight over the door, newspaper stuck in a missing pane. The land nearby was grown to bushes, but it was plain to see that the farm had been prosperous a hundred years ago. In back a barn had collapsed; maybe an old farmer, making poverty's choice, had stopped shingling the barn but kept a good roof on his house until the day he died.

Alexander stepped onto the front porch, feeling like an explorer, or an archeologist cutting away vines with his machete to find the Mayan temple. Davis lingered a yard behind. Alexander looked through a window at furniture standing in a parlor, dust hairy all over it. Through another window he saw the dining-room table, frayed oilcloth on it, with a plate and a coffee cup covered with something white: spiderwebs? mold? He shuddered and thought of the *Marie Celeste*, that intact and deserted ship that floated without direction on the sea; and of the train men found in the Rockies after the snow melted with its passengers vanished forever. In a few years this house would be another cellar-hole north of Tanglewood: a heap of bricks from the chimney; some broken shingles and rotten boards among blackberry bushes. Now it poised between house and no-house, a halo of dandelion seed waiting for the wind or a boy's breath.

With their fishing gear they walked to the edge of the brook, Alexander leading, and looked for an open spot to cast from. Bushes grew close to the water. They walked between the brook and the collapsed timbers of the barn with its mounds of black hay. They walked past the ruins of the farm shop, forge and millstone recognizable, past a sinking saphouse where farmers had kept fire going under the maple sap in winters of the Civil War. Then everything was bush; the branches were still wet, and their wet shirts clung to their bodies. They found a sandy spot to stand on, the stream dark and moving fast. Alexander fitted a worm on Davis's hook and Davis delicately dropped it near a rock that shelved out from the bank. A quick green-brown speckled shape flicked from the shadow of the ledge, nibbled at the worm, and flicked back. Alexander was puzzled; something was wrong. When he had walked here with his grandfather, he had caught brown trout or he had caught rainbows. These fish weren't the same.

A few more tries, and nothing. Davis pointed upstream and looked quizzically at his father. Alexander nodded and they picked their way upstream. His excitement grew. It was as if no one had fished this stream for years; as if no one had *ever* fished it before; or as if he were an Indian returned to the land after the settlers died out, after the brief life of the farmhouses, watching the quick water after the rain, and the green-brown fish in the water. Green-brown. Alexander's puzzlement returned, and then he remembered something; he stuck his hand in the water, and it numbed with the cold. He remembered Luke telling him about brook trout and showing him an illustration in an old natural history book. In the old days brook trout had been native to the streams. Then the farmers came and cut down the trees to plough land and the temperature of the unshaded water rose by ten or fifteen degrees. The brook trout died off, and the brown trout and the rainbows that liked warmer water took over the stream. Now the farmers had died out and the woods had come back. There were bear again, plundering city people's compost-heaps, bear that had not dared to descend from the hilltops for two hundred years. And now the brook trout had come back—these had to be brook trout—under the shade of new pine.

Upstream they picked their way, both silent and absorbed, until they came upon a beaver dam. They fingered the workmanship of the new dam and saw the old gray one behind it. Then they pushed through a gate of bushes. Above the dam the brook widened into a round pool. Alexander could see where the brook entered at the other end and pointed it out to Davis. The swimming hole. This must have been the swimming hole for the children from the farm—and Lord knows how many farms there used to be. Alexander and Davis mounted the roots of a great oak, a little platform over the water, and Alexander baited their hooks, and both of them cast into the pool. Neither spoke. Birch trees crowded close to the edge of the pool, and beyond them the dark green of pines over the red floor. The birches leaned in toward the pool and the birch-tops gathered together, high up, as if smoke had grown leaves.

Davis's cork ducked firmly under the water. He made a faint breathing noise of excitement and reeled in; a vigorous small shape battled him in the water. Alexander put down his rod—though his cork was agitating also—and took a lithe, flopping, square-tailed brook trout off Davis's hook. Davis filled the sap bucket with cold water and Alexander dropped the fish in. He baited Davis's hook again and reeled in his own trout, and when he had dropped it in the bucket, Davis had caught another.

Alexander set his own rod back against the trunk of the oak; one fisherman was enough. Davis let out little giggles of excitement and Alexander looked at him with easy affection. The boy's mouth hung open in a grin and he looked more abandoned, more given-up-to-something, than at any time Alexander could remember. Maybe in two weeks' time they could come back again to this very place. The pool was so beautiful, dim in the woody twilight of gray birch; only a corner of sunlight moved through the frail trunks and twigs. It was as if they were under water and the birches were weeds under water and Alexander and Davis breathed the thick air of the water. I must remember the brook trout, thought Alexander—this cold, old flesh that numbed his fingers was the past returning, the dead replaced by older dead. For a moment he felt an elation that reminded him of the false elation of drunkenness the night before; maybe, he let himself think, it need not be false.

Davis tentatively baited a hook himself. Then with more confidence he wrestled a trout from hook to bucket and baited again. Alexander smiled—and smiled at his faint resentment, being superseded. He stood on the roots of the oak, floating on his sense of the whole scene: pool, birches, black water. Davis moved on the sandy fringe at the water's edge and approached the top of the pool where the water entered. Alexander was aware that they had to leave soon. Soon they must load themselves up and take the trout home to Elizabeth in Lincoln on the highway full of weekenders returning and drive to Boston and tomorrow the group life contract. But now he stood on the oak's root by a pool in the Ben Watts Brook that was crowded with brook trout and that no one had fished for ages, miles from anyone, years from anyone, and in two weeks . . .

A noise interrupted his thoughts. Annoyed, he looked toward the end of the pool where Davis stood rigid making a high eerie sound, a small steady keening that, Alexander suddenly shook himself to realize, was the sound of terror. Had he caught the hook in his eye? Alexander jumped from the root to the edge of the stream and splashed through the freezing water to Davis's side. Davis was staring.

Alexander picked up the angle of his sight and saw a pile of old clothes with a fishing rod sticking out of it. Then he saw the arm, bone mostly with brown strips of skin sticking to it, a mass of ants digging into the remaining meat of the forearm. The skull was thrown back and wedged between birches, the eyes and the lips gone, a few ants scouring bone and shredded cheek. Through a hole in the overalls more colonies of ants pursued their labor. One hand that lay loose on the needled dirt was stripped of flesh entirely and lay delicately flopped, finger bones articulate and sensible, still holding together.

Davis turned, dropping his rod, and ran into the woods, loud cries coming from the small body. Alexander ran after him, caught him, and carried the shuddering body through bushes that scraped face and arms, to the car, past the house of the dead fisherman, to the road, to the highway, and east toward metropolitan Boston. Davis lay with face pressed into Alexander's shoulder and sobbed as Alexander patted and caressed him, until after a while he noticed that Davis was asleep.

The rain started again as the car drove itself through the monotony of the dark turnpike. Wipers moved back and forth and Alexander watched miles of returning cars ahead of him, headlights sinking down into a valley and climbing a long hill. Without wanting to, he saw the cars as a line of ants crawling into and out of the body of the dead man in the woods. So he had to think about it.

Why hadn't anybody missed him? Was there an old sister or widow alive and incontinent next to Sarah in the home at Hubert's Falls? Was there a granddaughter in Spokane who wondered why postcards had stopped coming? What about the rural delivery mailman, the tax collector, the old neighbors stopping for an annual visit on a summer Sunday? Or was there—he realized—no one at all?

So he was the one to bury the dead, closest kin by the accident of Davis's discovery. Maybe one day Alexander himself would die alone and without anyone to miss him. He shook his head abruptly as the mosquito of self-pity buzzed around him looking for a place to land. What should he *do*? He should telephone or write someone. There must be a constable for the town; he knew there were selectmen. But how could he identify himself and tell them the story without seeming stupid and callous to have run away? Of course it was the only thing he could have done, considering Davis. He let his hand move from the steering wheel to rest on his son's frail neck. Davis's neck and shoulder shuddered like a horse's, and Alexander moved his hand back to the wheel. He knew what he would do; he would write a note addressed "Constable or First Selectman" to the town of New Harbor and tell about the body and draw a map to show where it was. He would not sign the note.

He had solved his problem and heaviness left him. He started rehearsing the conference tomorrow with Sol Reitman on the contract for the new group life. In his mind's small theater he spoke wittily and brightly, and they went off to lunch and a pair of Bloody Marys. Then he looked down at Davis's wet sleeping face and saw that his glasses had fallen off, and he thought how the brook trout would die in the sap bucket in the woods when they had used up the oxygen in the water.

EMBARRASSMENT

A constable walked up and down on the pavement below the open window. Inside, the party of eight had finished dinner and sat drinking brandy by the windows overlooking the park. Someone in the room suggested that they each tell the most embarrassing thing that had ever happened to them. The hostess spoke first, while her husband who owned newspapers in Brazil poured more brandy from the bottle that he said he had found at Christie's. The hostess was tall, still young, of a provenance subject to conjecture, and she told of entering an American courtroom for her first divorce when she was nineteen, wearing a skirt that wrapped and tied around her waist; as she followed her lawyer toward the bench, the skirt caught on a doorknob and peeled off. Fortunately, she said, she was wearing underpants.

When everyone had finished laughing, the novelist and the film producer each spoke at the same moment. They deferred to each other, until finally the novelist, who was English, persuaded the film producer to speak first. He was a tiny, dried-up man, Italian, who wore a yellow linen suit and a green ascot. He spoke of meeting a celebrated actress as she entered her middle years, while he was still an assistant director. He was so nervous that he drank more than he was accustomed to and proved incapable of demonstrating his affection when they retired for the evening. He woke to hear her screaming in a Neapolitan dialect of which she possessed perfect command. He had urinated in his sleep over the silk sheets of her bed and over the great woman herself.

The novelist waited for silence before he began his story. He spoke emphatically, with much facial expression, and the rest of the party paid scrupulous attention. "I came up to London on a Sunday evening," he said, "to have lunch the next day, the matter of a Thames contract. . . . In the evening I strolled in the park, naturally enough, and encountered an attractive young man—an American—rather butch, blond with tight jeans. We returned to my hotel and soon enough we were at it. Not to put too fine a point upon it, I was buggering him, when he made a most satisfactory little cry into the pillow and shook with a great frisson—which quite finished me off. But when I rolled off, I discovered that he was dead.

"My erotic powers may not be held accountable, flattering as that might be. The fellow had clearly suffered a heart attack. At first I was quite cross about it. How thoughtless of him! Maupassant has a story about a wife whose lover dies in her bed just as her husband is expected. At least she could enlist the aid of the town doctor. . . .

"I hadn't the faintest notion of his name. He had been cautious enough not to carry any identification, not a key or a wallet. Obviously I could not leave him in the room for which I had registered. I had to remove him, which meant that I had first to *clothe* the sod. It took me an hour to stretch the blue jeans on. The T-shirt was simple but the cowboy boots! . . . And when I had dressed him, *then* what did I have?

"There was no hope of carrying him and simply pretending he was drunk. Outside, in the hallway, I found a table on wheels, the sort they use for room service. I put him on it and wheeled him down the hall into a laundry room with great cabinets full of towels and bedding. As luck would have it there was a capacious chute for soiled linen. I helped him into it, and he fell without making a sound.

"I checked out, took an early train to Kent, telephoned Hilary to tell him that I was ill and, awfully sorry, must cancel lunch. . . . Then indeed I was ill.

"But I heard no more of it."

After the company had laughed and expressed their shock, everyone agreed that the novelist's predicament had been most embarrassing. The five who had not yet told stories protested that they could not possibly follow him. The host, the tall, white-haired Brazilian, waited a minute, as if thinking, then opened another bottle. On the pavement below the open windows, the constable paused and listened to the merriment above. Then he shook his head and began walking again.

REVIVALS

Three men talked at 2:00 A.M. in the living room of a cheap suite at the Hotel Cherokee on Forty-fourth Street across from the Algonquin. Until midnight they had rehearsed a revival of Ben Higbee's *Scrapiron Ballad*, which would open in four weeks at the Theatre de Lys. The old playwright asked his producer, Louis, and his director, Colin, back to the Cherokee for brandy, excusing his invitation by saying that early rehearsals were the time for talk. Really, he asked them because he had been a widower for only five months and had trouble sleeping.

They had almost finished the small bottle, swishing Martells in cloudy tumblers. They talked the play over for the hundredth time; they agreed on their approach to the production, and agreed also about certain worries. Colin used the phrase "period piece" too often for Ben's comfort. Then, when they had gone over an ingenue's interpretation, they began to talk about women.

Louis's third marriage was in trouble. It was his own fault, he admitted. He lost himself to infatuations with young women who acted in his plays. "I've showed I'm *sincere*," he mocked himself, "I married two of them." By this time, he said, his analyst's eyebrows discouraged him from pleading love. "Why, damn it, is somebody new always erotic? It's ridiculous." He shook his head. He had recently turned forty and gained weight; his gray suit was too small for him, and on the ring finger of his left hand a gold band sank into puffy flesh.

Ben had liked Louis immediately. He wasn't so sure about Colin, who was even younger than Louis and who had just stopped calling him Professor Higbee. Thin with nerves, Colin crossed and uncrossed his legs in their tight jeans and smiled like a sign switching on and off. He said that after an early divorce he had remained single; in the theater, he said, it was easy to marry and difficult to stay that way. He made the announcement casually while he chain-smoked Camels.

Ben remarked that *he* had stayed married a long time—but, then, he had lived mostly outside the theater. After the one success of *Scrapiron* in the late forties, as they knew, he had taught playwrighting at a university for thirty years. When he was young and theatrical, it was true, there had been a brief first marriage. "But Lucille and I were together twenty-eight years," he said as if he were only providing information. After a pause he mentioned again that the revival of his play came at a fortunate time; he frankly admitted that he was lonely.

As they talked, sleepily, Louis tried defining "erotic" as he had used it. He meant something other than sexuality itself, or the wild pleasure that took place between people used to each other, even between wives and husbands, familiar enough to ignore romance, conquest, secrecy, illegitimacy, contrivance —"All that glorious bullshit," Louis said.

Colin told a story from the year he spent with the Berliner Ensemble. He had known artists from all over East Germany.

"They were all anti-regime, some way or other. When you got them alone." He sipped his brandy. "The old ones had been underground during the war. Or so they claimed. Some were Marxists, socialist anti-Communists. Some weren't political especially, or doctrinaire anyway, but resented the censorship. Or repression of any kind. So they printed underground magazines on old ozolid copying machines and circulated poems and stories against the regime, or stuff that the regime called formalist. They met secretly, they carried novels in briefcases, microfilm in hollowed-out canes . . . Super-spy stuff." Colin paused; then he smirked: "They were all faithful to their wives."

Louis nodded his head vigorously. "We grew up lying to our parents, so we go on lying the rest of our lives. Keeps you young," he said.

"Because they betrayed the regime," said Colin.

"But the *most* lies," said Louis, wringing his fat hands and sighing, "are the ones we believe in the most—the same thing over and over again. I carry an erratum slip on my forehead: 'For love read hate throughout, for hate read love.' "

They were silent for a moment. Ben remembered a story he could tell, then thought better of it. When Colin looked at his watch Ben felt loneliness roll from the room's corners, and he interrupted Louis who was about to speak. "When we listed things—secrecy, conquest, illegitimacy—we left one thing out."

Louis emptied the brandy bottle into his glass.

"Hatred," said the playwright. "What you said: 'For love read hate throughout . . .' " He borrowed from Colin the first cigarette he had touched in ten years; he set his tumbler hard on the table splashing drops of cognac on the plastic surface. "I remember something that happened not long after the war. I don't even remember her name."

He wanted to speak well, to keep their attention. He heard himself varying pitch and pause like a bad actor auditioning.

"She was married to a man I knew at college. She was Danish but she'd lived everywhere—beautiful, with fine distinct small features. When I first saw her I felt the breath go out of me. I've felt that way only two or three times in my life. Do you remember that Chekhov story about the two beauties?"

Colin nodded. Ben paused to light the Camel and after one puff coughed harshly and put it out. He wiped his eyes and went on. "Modeling took her back and forth—London, New York. When she talked that night, she kept referring to periods or places in her life that made her sound a thousand years old. She looked, oh, twenty-seven maybe. We were choosing dessert at a Jewish restaurant in Rome, and when I picked baklava, she tossed off, 'A Romanian husband I once married'—usually her English sounded native—'*adored* baklava.' She started to tell a story but Basil interrupted her. I had known this man slightly in college, Basil Peabody, though we moved in different sets. Basil shook his head from side to side, stared across at me, and spoke with an attempt at the epigram—which was his manner, and he wasn't very good at it. 'The gentleman in question,' he said, 'was neither Romanian nor her husband.'"

Colin drained his tumbler, put out one Camel and lighted another. Louis had finished his brandy, and from the inside pocket of his coat he pulled out a pint of Wild Turkey, loosened the cap, and set it on the table.

"Although he spoke softly, I could tell he was enraged—I suppose because of something that had happened earlier, I don't know. . . . His cheeks were red-blue, like the maroon tie he wore, almost purple, and I realized that he was drunk as well as furious.

"I sat in the booth next to the Danish woman. Inge! Her name just came to me. Thirty-seven years ago! . . . The booth was small and we were squeezed together. Basil sat opposite her. I thought he was a clod when I knew him at college; now I realized that his feelings for me were cooler than mine for him. I don't know why. . . . He was rich and I was successful; probably he wanted to write novels, though not enough to do anything about it. Sitting next to him, across from me in the little booth, was my wife Martha—my *then* wife, as they say—who had not spoken since we sat down except when she exclaimed over the little fried artichokes we had for hors d'oeuvres. Delicious things.

"She was so young, Martha. Twenty-one years old." Ben shook his head. "I was twenty-eight or -nine, I suppose. We were not getting on, not at all. I was full of myself in those days, and she was no bargain. Yes, I remember; she did say one thing. After Inge mentioned the husband who adored baklava, and after Basil's epigram, there was a pause in our conversation, naturally enough. I broke the silence by praising baklava and Martha contradicted me: Baklava was *dreadful*; the honey made the pastry soggy. That was all; nobody answered her; it was stupidly typical, of both of us. It doesn't have to be like that. . . . "

His mind suddenly filled with Martha's face as it had looked when he packed to leave the apartment on Twelfth Street, a year after Rome—her face bloated and red-raw with tears, begging him not to go.

He returned to his story, forcing himself to speak with animation. "When she met Inge and Basil at the restaurant, Martha hated them both. Instantly. It was a way of getting at me; these were supposed to be my friends. She kept silent, icy, making her boredom as obvious as she could." He sighed again, looking at the mottled backs of his hands, spreading out his long fingers. Colin crossed and uncrossed his legs.

"But of course she disliked Inge's type, also—someone whose life developed entirely from beauty and fashion. You understood: a series of rich men. We knew some of the American crowd in Rome and Paris, writers and would-be writers from rich New York families. Women like Inge joined the set, wandered out again. Cannes, Gstaad . . . There were others in Rome. That was the year we spent at the Academy.

"After Basil contradicted her about the Romanian husband, she did something extraordinary. After I ordered baklava and the waiter disappeared, I looked sideways at Inge and found myself pierced by a smile so tender, so intimate, that I almost melted into a baklava myself. She laughed as if Basil had made a pleasantry and leaned so that her shoulder touched mine. To my surprise I felt myself responding under the table. I discovered her 'eroticism,' as we call it, not in my eyes or in my mind but in my trousers.

"Then she told her story. I can't remember a word but it was about the pseudo-Romanian. She told it with great vivacity, waving her right hand, mimicking accents, supplying sound effects—while Martha glared past my ear, looking as bored as she could manage, and Basil gazed into his drink with his eyes half-closed. Inge gestured with her right hand because with her left hand she was beating me off under the table."

Louis and Colin let out whoops of surprise, boyish noises in the early morning of the hotel room. Ben heard melancholy in the sounds. He heard his own voice pretending to lightness.

"Needless to say she was subtle about it. When the waiter set down the baklava—espresso for the women, a drink for Basil—she unzipped my fly and slipped her hand through the vent in my boxer shorts. While she worked, the upper part of her arm never jiggled. She talked wildly, gesturing with her right hand while her left hand performed under the table, and I quickly reached the most erotic few seconds of my life—as my wife Martha looked past me unknowing, as this Basil-husband stared into his Galliano while two feet away Inge cuckolded him."

When the younger men finished laughing, Louis poured himself a finger of Wild Turkey. No one spoke for a minute.

Martha's young face returned to Ben, pinched and white in the courtroom, the old lawyer shuffling beside her with his hand on her elbow; and he remembered the astonishment with which he had suddenly felt both jealousy and intolerable loss.

"I almost choked eating the baklava," he went on. "When I sighed it passed for a compliment to the pastry chef." He sighed again, feeling an ocean of depression roll toward him, thinking: I have just bragged like an eighteen-year-old. "Of course it was anger, hatred, that prompted her"—he continued, unable to stop—"and that made it so delicious for me. There was nothing between us. She was beautiful, yes, but I didn't even know her. At the time I wondered if she was interested in theatrical connections—but she was interested only in setting horns on Basil's head. What I didn't know, of course, was that I loathed Martha . . . and that's why I found the moment so exquisite."

Louis nodded vigorously at this confirmation. Colin looked at his watch again, pulled out another Camel and put it back.

"Because I was young and stupid I thought that I was in love with her. For a few days anyway. I wanted to take her to a hotel on some Roman side street. But she had no interest in me. When I spoke to her outside the restaurant she pretended not to understand. I never saw her again."

After a silence Ben yawned, struggling not to, a yawn repeated by Louis and Colin in tandem. Louis said that he had to get home and Colin stood up and stretched, nodding. Rehearsal would not begin until 5:00 P.M., to accommodate an actress who worked in a soap, but in the meantime there were details of costumes and set. Louis had other matters to attend to, not to mention the hour with his analyst. Louis poured Ben some Wild Turkey to take to bed, then put the bottle back in his inside pocket.

As the three men stood up, Ben spoke again. "Basil's been dead twenty years. Last year Martha retired from practicing law, a profession she hadn't dreamed of, that year in Rome. I just heard that she has Parkinson's. I wonder if Inge is alive. . . .

"And here am I," he said, laughing faintly, shrugging his shoulders, as he let the producer and director out the door.

"And here am I," he said aloud when he was alone again. He looked out the window at dingy brick in the airshaft. When he turned out the light, quick scenes shifted back and forth between Martha and Lucille. Inge's face rose before him, and for a second he tasted pastry flakes, walnuts, and honey. From the next room he heard a small dog's muffled bark, and a sleepy woman's voice that repeated, "Do you want to go out, Hector? Do you want to go out?"

THE

IDEAL

BAKERY

When I was a boy my father sometimes took me for breakfast to the Ideal Bakery on State Street just over the New Haven line from Hamden, where we ate the wonderful crullers that Gus and Ingrid Goetz made every morning.

The best memories go back before the war, to the spring of 1939 when I was ten years old, aware of Hitler and newsreel armies marching, aware that war was something for dreading. An only child at that time, I overheard my parents' worried talk: My father at thirty-five thought he would be drafted. When I was nine I had collected War Cards like the other boys, four-color images one-penny-each in a wax wrapper with a creased sheet of bubblegum pink as a heifer's tongue. These cards showed the Japanese bombing buses in China, bodies blowing apart, entrails scattering in air, but they were no more real than Ace Comics. Then one day in 1938 my mother took me to a matinee movie in New Haven, *The Dead in Barcelona*.

Probably she needed to do some shopping on a no-school day and took me with her offering the treat of a movie; she must have thought that it was a mystery because of *The Dead*. . . . As it turned out, I watched in horror as airplanes strafed refugees pulling carts stuffed with their belongings, their mouths making big O's as they screamed; women clutching babies collapsed with blood leaking from their mouths; parents died while their children watched. When I came home I threw away my War Card collection.

Doubtless I was a morbid child but my life contained many pleasant things. It was during those years that I began to love sports, football mostly. Yale players Larry Kelley and Clint Frank won the Heisman Trophy two years in a row. Autumn Saturdays, my mother and I sat on the living room sofa following the game on radio, broadcast from the Yale Bowl only a few miles away, while my father worked in his den on columns of figures.

The spring of 1939 was my last as an only child, for my mother was pregnant with my sister, Evelyn. Because she was restless late in her pregnancy, every Saturday and Sunday we took long rides in the Pontiac. With our car radio my father could pick up WOR and I came to love the calm cheerful voice of Red Barber reaching us all the way from New York City, telling us about the Brooklyn Dodgers. That was the year my mother began to follow baseball—so that a year later, when she spent her time with Evelyn, and when she had started to act strange, the Brooklyn Dodgers remained a ribbon binding my mother and me together, not only on weekends in the Pontiac but on summer weekday afternoons as she and I listened in the darkened living room and the baby slept. We heard the names of young players still in the Minor Leagues— Peewee Reese, Pete Reiser. . . .

But the best memories do not belong to sports or baby sisters or my mother. Probably the biggest concentration of Ideal

Bakery mornings took place while my mother was in the hospital having Evelyn—new mothers stayed in the hospital ten days or two weeks at that time—but the excursions had started earlier, maybe on Saturdays when my mother slept late, and continued afterwards, during the war and the long anxious time when she was ill. For six years she was either sick in bed, with somebody coming in to help with the baby, or off in the asylum while help at home expanded to take care of everybody. My father and I went to the Ideal Bakery during these nervous times but the feeling was not the same. It was anxious wartime, and we were conspirators not in warmth and safety but in an absence or even in danger.

The best memory begins with my father's gentle hand shaking my shoulder in the gray May darkness at 5:45 A.M. After breakfast he would bring me home to get me ready for school before he went to the office. He worked at the lumberyard my great-grandfather Bud had started. Bud died five years before I was born but I knew all about him: Civil War veteran who sawed up his own trees in his own backyard at his own watermill by his own millstream. My grandfather Charlie built the yard up from a one-man shop until he employed twenty-three people and became "C.W.," the stern cigar-smoking boss (a self-made man, people said) while my father and his brother-in-law worked as co-managers in the office. I knew that my father hated his job—hated C.W.'s sarcasm, hated the maneuvering of my Uncle Bert, Aunt Regina's husband, which always ended putting Bert in the right and my father in the wrong—because I heard him complain to my mother. I heard him weep in frustration. He hated his work so much that he was at his desk before eight o'clock six days a week and brought stacks of arithmetic home every night and on weekends.

But that hand on my shoulder, sweetly shaking me awake, carried nothing but affection with it and tender conspiracy. My mother at Grace-New Haven with the baby was somehow benignly tricked by our adventure, as my father and I performed commandolike a secret escapade or mission. I dressed quickly and carefully, tying my own shoes, and remembered to brush my hair. In the kitchen my father waited in his brown fedora, topcoat over the business suit always gray or brown, and the shined shoes always black. ("Meticulous" was a word he loved; he went to his barber once a week to have his thin hair trimmed.) He waited smiling the slightly tilted smile— slanted up on the left side of his mouth with its large skin-mole—that was the grin of our father-and-son conspiracy. Pontiac keys dangled from his right hand.

The windshield steamed those mornings. His gloved hands wiped clean the glass fogged with our breaths as he pulled out the choke, slipping it back gradually, and we rolled quietly through the streets of small houses where my schoolmates, never so lucky, slept until their mothers woke them to Ralston or Post Toasties. My father grinning beside me enjoyed these breakfasts as much as I did, and in the early morning he was energetic and optimistic. Often he sang in his high sweet tenor as he drove—"My Blue Heaven," sometimes, or songs his grandfather brought back from the Civil War and sang to my baby-father: one about "campfires burning" (war in olden times) and another sweetly sad: "Backward, turn backward, O time in thy flight! Make me a child again, just for tonight!"

When we reached Whitney Avenue my father accelerated. Early traffic was light, and we cut over the Lake Whitney bridge by the long icehouses and headed for State Street. We bumped over tracks past workers waiting for trolleys and in a mile or two parked by the Ideal Bakery. We held hands as we walked from the car to the shiny black-and-ivory glass front, then dropped them as we came to the door. Inside we saw Gus himself standing at the cash register—a redheaded man in his forties, a fierce protective figure, stern but not frightening, righteous and dignified—who welcomed us warmly without smiling and motioned us toward a booth. Always I stared first, to get it over with, at the red birthmark between his right eye and ear, as red as his hair and shaped like the trylon of the trylon-and-perisphere at the New York World's Fair. I could tell that my father admired Gus, in the way that good men find of trusting one another. It was clear that Gus felt the same way about my father, and some of this regard spilled onto me when Gus, in a quiet half-minute, would stop by the booth and say: "Well, look at that boy! Well, I'll be darned!"

The regard that the two men felt for each other, as I assembled it from bits and pieces, had a history that came out of business and bad times. Back in 1932 or 1933, when a nickel cruller or cup of coffee was a luxury for Gus's customers, my father let Gus take some building materials on credit—at his own risk, without telling my grandfather. Gus paid my father back at fifty cents a week until he had a good month in 1936. Then Gus paid the balance all at once, and at Christmas an unordered gross of crullers showed up at the lumberyard for the workers to take home to their families.

When Gus spoke of "that boy"—me twisting, smiling, avoiding his gaze—my father asked about Augustus, Jr., called Dutch at school but not at the Ideal Bakery, whom I saw on Saturday visits when he worked with his father. Dutch was a big boy, three years older than me, who boxed in amateur bouts at the YMCA. I hero-worshiped Dutch Goetz, just enough older, who worked with Gus as I would grow up to work with my father, making the fourth generation at the lumberyard. (So I thought.) Dutch scowled like his father under his abundant red hair, taller and strong-looking; already at fourteen he carried a dignity like his father's. In four years he would be drafted into the army, if he didn't join the marines first. My father and Gus talked about these alternatives while I listened knowing that in seven or eight years I would face the same choices; the war would go on forever and I would be part of it.

Gus was proud of Junior and of his daughter, Clara, who was older than Dutch and pretty, a cheerleader already as a high school sophomore, who worked as cashier on weekends and holidays. I could never determine how Gus felt about Ingrid, who was Mrs. Gus, and who waited on table. I never asked my father about it because I didn't want to ask, "Don't they *love* each other?" It puzzled me that they were so formal. When Gus wanted Ingrid to bring coffee to a customer, he wouldn't jab his fingers at the cup, the way they did in other places, or call her honeybunch and make people laugh: Gus would raise his voice politely, moderate his scowl, and say with a rising intonation, "Mrs. Goetz?" I suppose they worked together twelve or fifteen hours a day, year after year, and out of character and closeness evolved this formality.

My young father—it startles me that he was only thirty-five years old—sat with me in a green booth, our hats and jackets and topcoats over the poles that separated the seats. My father's thick white mug of coffee steamed in front of him while I drank a large glass of Brock-Hall milk and each of us ate three crullers.

Oh, the light still-warm delicate crisp gently greasy blonde unsugared braids of dough! The first bite was the best, and my father and I looked into each other's eyes as we first bit into the tender sweet crust that "melted in the mouth" as my father put it, and we grinned with a pleasure greater even than our anticipation. When I finished the second cruller my ten-year-old stomach was full but my mouth could not deny itself the third. My father swallowed another cup of coffee, which Ingrid poured while she heard us for the thousandth time praise her crullers. She told us again how she and Gus arrived every morning at 4:00 A.M. to get things going, how she stirred the batter just so, how Gus cut the strips and how they braided them together. Then the Greek arrived at six-thirty and heated the oil and turned crullers out for the customers, fresh batches every few minutes. Yes, she agreed, they *were* the best crullers she had ever tasted, if she said so herself. . . .

My father and I talked and he smiled without nervousness or anxiety. Those mornings, I suppose no longer than half an hour at a time, we talked about Yale after Larry Kelley and Clint Frank; we talked about the Dodgers, whether Hot Potato Hamlin could keep on winning and maybe stop throwing the gopherball. Then my father would look at his wristwatch and the old nervy or frightened look would come over his face. Breakfast was over when he looked at his watch. As he drove me back to the house and then to school, we were still good companions talking about the Dodgers (or hockey, or football) but I knew that the lumberyard had taken over.

That's my story, no story at all: A boy and his father eat crullers. Then, of course, other things happen, predictable things. Ancient history is my hobby, and I think of a story Herodotus told, which Plutarch repeated and Cicero: Solon the Athenian lawgiver visited King Croesus, richest man in the world, who displayed for Solon his unimaginable wealth. He expected Solon to be envious but Solon was not: He told Croesus that we may call no man happy until he is dead. Later when Cyrus defeated Croesus and captured his treasure and chained him to the stake to burn him alive, he heard Croesus murmur: "Solon . . . Solon . . ."

It is impertinent to disagree with Cicero but I claim that the story makes Solon a simpleton. Everybody knows that the rich and the poor, the content and the discontent, the virtuous and the wicked burn at the same stake. Maybe once in a hundred lives, someone drops dead the day after signing her will or at the end of his active life or without pain or just before noticing the first sign of senility. When this good fortune happens, once in a hundred lives, there is no reason for it. Maybe Solon meant that no one should ever be counted happy—but if that's what he meant, Plutarch and Cicero misunderstood him.

The year I was a sophomore in high school—four years after Evelyn was born, when my mother was still depressed, taking electroshock treatments in the mental hospital—we gathered in the auditorium one morning to watch the school heavy-weight boxing finals. (Our wartime physical fitness program had us boxing every day in gym class.) I was excited that day because my friend Dutch Goetz, about to graduate and join the marines, was a finalist. A big blond football player from a rich neighborhood knocked him out in the second round. One blow lifted Dutch off his feet and onto the ropes and he slumped to the floor like a collapsing sack. I had never seen anyone knocked out before, and I was shocked, and I think that my continual recollection of this collapse left me less shocked, six months later in November, when we heard the cottony sound of the school PA come on at an unusual time, and the principal's pompous, somber voice announce with re-gret that Augustus Goetz, Jr., Class of 1943, had been killed in action in the second wave invading Tarawa.

At this time my mother was out of her mind and I was cared for by a succession of crabby widows while my father looked sadder and sadder and went out alone Saturday nights and came home drunk, as the widows never failed to tell me. Sometimes he drank at home but not often, and sometimes he stopped drinking and took me again to the Ideal Bakery, where the crullers were as good as ever, but now nothing tasted so good as it had tasted before, and Gus's mouth turned further down, and he never said, "Look at the boy." Some-times Ingrid was sarcastic now and their daughter married and went to Ohio.

After the war ended my mother was well enough to come

home, and she gradually strengthened, but as she got stronger my father's head and hands started to shake, kidney failure and uremic poisoning, and he died at forty-five when I was a sophomore at college and Evelyn a fifth-grader. A month after my father died, my mother sent me a clipping about the death, at forty-seven, after a long illness, of Mrs. Augustus Goetz, formerly of the Ideal Bakery. Later I found out that Gus had sold the bakery to the Greek in order to nurse Ingrid at home and had used up the money that they had accumulated over their years of fifteen-hour days. When she died he went to work making crullers for the Greek, and the Ideal Bakery turned into the Akropolis Café. It's torn down now.

Last week I saw Gus again. My mother, despite her troubles in middle life, is alive in her right mind at eighty-five. My sister, Evelyn, died last year of breast cancer and my mother survived even that, as she survived my son's crippling injury in a motorcycle accident when he was sixteen. (I do not mean that we have suffered more than anyone else. Of course there were years without disaster, even decades with few losses.) But her arthritis keeps her in a wheelchair in a nursing home and she is catheterized all the time. I visit her on Wednesdays and Saturdays; sometimes we watch football or baseball together on a Saturday. I knew from her, maybe a month ago, that Gus Goetz had been admitted, ninety years old and senile. Last week I saw him in the corridor, smaller but still wiry, the same strawberry trylon between his right eye and ear. He was almost naked, the hospital gown pulled up, and he screamed at the orderlies who tried to subdue him, "Shit! Shit!" in a fierce old croak. His face and hands were covered with excrement, which he tried to eat.

My mother lives in daily pain, unable to tolerate medication, but her mind remains good. My mind is good also, and although a few physical problems have turned up, I will probably live many years. Was Dutch the lucky one? My father?

Not Evelyn nor Ingrid, I'm sure. My mother? All and none, I suppose. Like everybody I live in many places and they are all inside my head. I cannot believe that this is avoidable or that it should be avoided. Several times a week I am ten years old sitting in a booth at the Ideal Bakery, loving my tender father who smiles across the tabletop. He has not begun to shake; Evelyn is unborn, ungrown, undead; Dutch grows fiercer; the Dodgers look ahead to Reese and Reiser returning from the war; I taste again the twisted light warm dough.

MRS.

THING

Her new flat on Fitzhugh Square resembled the old one in Kensington, not just for the familiar sofa and Piranesi's "Temple of Diana," but because it repeated the old flat's air of scatter and improvisation. For three years he had mailed infrequent air-letters to this address from his office in the Department of Romance Languages; it had been five years, what with many expenses including a divorce, since he had visited the London where they had been lovers. Doubtless it was chancy to look her up again. He assured himself that it was curiosity that brought him here, together with something like friendship; it was not old love.

"When I last saw you," Rosalind was saying, "you looked *most* morose. Do you remember? I doubt you remember." He had given up trying to answer her questions. "You left me occupying a window seat in an airplane at Logan Airport in Boston, if you recollect, because your *wife* was waiting for you at the gate, doubtless with one or more of your *children*—whom you could not bear to leave, as of course I understood perfectly, and who made your divorce impossible. I was to fly to New York on the same plane, and back to London." She swallowed some whiskey. "Which I dutifully did."

Ned Hightower sat on the pale green sofa watching Rosalind's mouth move in rapid speech. Her modeled lips, sensuous and sculptural, enunciated with their familiar cool clarity. She was doing nicely at thirty-four—although tonight she was angry and moderately drunk. On his arrival she had presented him with an inch of whiskey in a wineglass, and he had noted that the pint bottle was a third gone. In Kensington, when they had been together, she was always rushing to find pound-notes in an old mackintosh, counting change from her purse, then dashing to a pub to buy a bottle just before a visitor arrived. Her blonde hair was straight then, molded around her handsome skull; now it curled abundantly.

She rose to refill his glass, emptying the bottle, and gestured toward the plate of cheeses. He spooned Stilton onto a Bath Oliver and ate a sprig of celery. "I quite believed you," she went on, "when you discovered the impossibility of divorce. You communicated your epiphany by air-letter, as you may recall, some months after our parting in Boston. After all, I had been first to announce that you would not divorce. On the many occasions when you told me that your love was without historical precedent, that you would leave your family and move into my flat, that you would resign your university and work in London as a free-lance translator, I told you that you mustn't. I told you indeed that you wouldn't."

At the time of their love affair, she had been twenty-nine and he thirty-seven. She was quite right, of course, in her recollections. Although she had loved him—and spent her savings to fly to Los Angeles for an impetuous American weekend—she had continually and calmly insisted that he was incapable of leaving his children. Finally he had come to agree with her, although he considered at the time that he loved Rosalind with unsurpassable passion. That was before he had met someone else and decided that he had been fooling himself about Rosalind. As he listened to her anger, he tried out the notion that she had fooled herself also: There had been other men beside him, of course, even serious love affairs—and yet she had never married. Surely it was not coincidental that she loved only bisexuals or married men? If she indeed had loved him, five years ago, and claimed that she *wanted* to marry him, doubtless she had known that he was safe. . . .

And what, after all, he thought in a familiar refrain, was *love*? Five years ago he had expressed himself on the subject without diffidence.

"It is just as well that Richard is in Cornwall," she was saying, "or I would not see you here. Simply for the awkwardness. He is I suppose more tenant than lover. At any rate he is eclectic in his erotic tastes, as I am sure Derek told you." She had nearly emptied her glass. "Flats are expensive and I do not work all the time."

He had ventured at first, like a polite acquaintance, to ask about her work. She had stared back at him for a moment, but had delivered the form of an answer: Work was about the same; parts for radio—a play, or reading a book aloud—were steadiest, as they had always been. Once a year there might be a television series, which contributed most to the exchequer. Now and again she was offered a role at a provincial theater—never the West End, never films. . . . "Canterbury," she said. "Perhaps you remember Canterbury?"

Five years ago, just before his return to the States, they had spent a week at a small hotel in Canterbury while she rehearsed *Lysistrata* from ten to five. It was a week in which he assured her that he would return as soon as he arranged for divorce, and she assured him that he would not. Every morning they woke turning to each other to make love, then lingered in bed until it was late, so that she ran to rehearsal carrying bread and butter, her short skirt bouncing as she looked back, chewing and waving—although in England, as she told him, eating outdoors was not permitted. She looked so touching, so beautiful, as she ran off to work eating her breakfast; it bothered him not at all that she clearly knew the figure she cut.

When she returned late in the afternoon they would have a drink in their room and make love again before dinner. Every night the same waiter paid them elaborate court; they teased each other over which of them the waiter lusted after. Rosalind claimed that it was Ned's accent that made him so irresistible, as he ordered in offensively correct French from a Calabrian. They sat with brandy in the lounge after dinner, and he day-dreamed aloud about their life together in Kensington when he returned after his divorce. Mostly she let him ramble on; now and then she disputed his premise. Often, he remembered, he had discoursed at length on the nature of love. Months later in Los Angeles—that desperate weekend he had seen her last—he remembered how they had walked on bleak Hollywood Boulevard stepping on stars as he monologued, unable in his panic to stop talking about *love*. . . .

Tonight they found a cab to take them to L'Haricot Vert on Greek Street —none of the old haunts, thank you— and in the flurry of settling into the cab Rosalind was silent for a moment. She shuddered in the damp November cool. Ned asked: "Do you see Derek?"

Possibly it was not the most tactful question; possibly, Ned thought, that was why he asked it. Derek was their mutual friend, as it were, the theatrical literary agent who had repre-sented Ned's adaptation of Molière. Five years ago the two men had taken lunch together at the Salisbury. Rosalind ap-peared delighted and surprised to encounter her old friend De-rek, who of course introduced her to Ned, who was immediately taken with her spectacular carved head and her sensuous, well-spoken mouth. Later, on request, Derek discovered Rosalind's telephone number in his theatrical black book as if he were surprised to find it. It took Ned two weeks of telephone calls—lunches, drinks, and progressive infatuation—to discover that Derek, also married of course, was Rosalind's current lover; the Salisbury encounter had been arranged.

By that time Ned was far too dedicated in his pursuit to feel scruples about a friend's friend. For that matter, he knew that discreet Derek always kept something going on the side, while the proper wife and three children waited at home. Perhaps he had rather envied Derek his worldly arrangements; at any rate, he had not only emulated his friend, he had cut him out. Because Rosalind would not indulge more than one lover at a time, she dropped Derek for Ned. Derek had been annoyed. One of his colleagues had marketed Ned's adaptation.

Another element in the tactlessness of his question was Derek's visit to Boston a year earlier. It had marked a reconciliation for the two men. When Derek stayed at Ned's bachelor flat, he heard about a woman who lived in Newton.

"How *dear* of you to ask," said Rosalind. "You have always been so loyal a friend to him—as have we all—but then your record of loyalty is consistent, is it not?"

Ned understood that he had offered her this opportunity. He smiled to himself as the taxi entered Soho, where he remembered reading advertisements in shop windows: MISS WHIPPELASHE CORRECTION ADMINISTERED IN GYM COSTUME.

"I *do* remember," she said, "your firmly held positions on love, loyalty, and fidelity, *my* fidelity of course, as you departed to return to your Boston wife and children, whom you would abandon shortly of course. Or again in Los Angeles on our transatlantic dirty weekend, when you occupied many *precious* hours, as you repeatedly called them, with your ridiculous jealousy. I took your convictions most seriously, of course. When I told you that I had lapsed, momentarily, during my affair with Derek, with that visiting Czech director, you were positively *stricken*," she said. "*Poor* dear. It took me three hours to convince you that I would remain nunlike in your absence."

He remembered that she had talked rather a lot about other men; did he remember encouraging her?

"I believe you understand quite well that Derek telephoned as soon as he returned to London from your 'pad,' as he mentioned that you disgustingly called it. Of course he could not delay to tell me about your divorce, and about the latest episode in your long history of fidelity. It took him five years to take his revenge. He was *so* pleased, dear Derek."

A headwaiter sat them against the wall of a narrow room before a tiny table. They ordered whiskeys and left their menus unopened.

"I regret to say that I was shocked," said Rosalind. "I am thirty-four years old, I have spent seventeen years in the theater, I have known a number of men—and I was *shocked*." The drinks interrupted her. "I am no longer shocked to be shocked. But *you*"—her fury returned—"are extraordinary. After *entreating* me to wait for you, after lecturing me interminably about love, after encouraging me in a midnight telephone call to fly to your country . . . *six weeks* after I returned to London, as Derek told me with considerable pleasure, you found yourself another dolly.

"There was an episode that I never mentioned. Five months after you left Canterbury"—he had booked his flight for her day off from rehearsals and they had taken the train to Charing Cross, a taxi to Victoria, the bus to Heathrow; he could see her, sitting tensely beside him wearing a short dress, white with vertical black stripes—"I visited a gay actor at his flat and we drank whiskey together. I thought it was *quite* safe because I had encountered him with a succession of his little friends. To my astonishment, I discovered that he was not entirely gay, not by any means, and the next day I was *hysterical*. For a year I woke up from nightmares of my infidelity to *you*. Even after you admitted that you would not leave your children, that we would see each other only upon your *frequent* visits to London." She laughed angrily, still beautiful, "I did not, of course, require myself to continue my slightly tarnished vow of chastity"—how did the English learn to say things like "slightly tarnished vow"?—"but there have not been many men. Rather few, actually—but one or two *extraordinary* sexual experiences. Did Derek tell you about the season I spent doing rep in the East? I sent you a postcard, of course. There was a Bengali painter, quite talented, a disgusting-looking little man, but *extraordinary* . . ."

A second drink arrived, and the waiter lingered nearby. They opened their menus. Rosalind recited "artichaut vinaigrette sole spinach with citron please" without looking at the waiter. Enjoying his French again, Ned ordered snails with a venison escalope and petits pois. After looking at the wine list he chose a bottle of Meursault Genevrieres.

"Obviously the 'Department Chairman' is a gentleman of means," said Rosalind. Her voice held the words out for inspection.

"Moderately," he said, "but divorces are dear." He enjoyed talking English to the English. "On the other hand the San Francisco Rep, the University of Utah, and a theater in Cincinnati all resurrected the Molière last spring. And there is an advance on a textbook. It is not a great deal of money but it will buy us a bottle of Meursault."

"How clever of you," she said. "Americans are clever, aren't they? At least the clever ones. Do you remember the time you telephoned me on the set of that rather bad Trollope novel?" She put her carved head back and laughed.

It had not been one of his clever moments. Calling her during rehearsals for an ITV serial, he had spoken to the actor who picked up the phone—paterfamilias in the series that Ned watched later in Boston. Momentarily flustered, Ned used the American idiom although he was aware of its English associations: "Is Rosalind Moore available?"

The elderly actor, whom Rosalind called "a dear old poof," played his feed with italic emphasis: "*Well, I don't . . . really . . . know. Perhaps I should inquire . . . of Miss Moore?*" The company, as she told him, made much of it.

Rosalind talked continually during hors d'oeuvres. She talked while smoking a cigarette between courses, which she had once told him was as *infra dig* as eating on the pavement. Before they finished their entrees they started a second bottle of Meursault. Ned dutifully ingested dry venison and watery peas; Rosalind ate half her sole, half a piece of French bread, and disturbed her spinach. She was still talking when they finished the wine, declined a wagonload of cheese and pastry, took coffee, and ordered Hennessey VSQ in enormous snifters.

"I don't *wish* to know her name," she said. "I know that she has a husband and many, many children. *Mrs. Thing*," she said. "I call her *Mrs. Thing* and that is quite enough for me. I understand from Derek that she dropped you in favor of her old husband and revolting children. Of course you have my deepest sympathy."

He looked at her admiringly. Maybe RADA teaches you how to speak like that, he thought—every syllable placed correctly, like a headwaiter arranging a salad, cucumber here and tomato there.

"I know *quite* what she looks like," she said, "with her fat children. Revolting," she said. "Enormous, sallow, wrinkled, and revolting. *Mrs. Thing*."

The memory of another image was painful; he shook it off. His mind returned to his latest definition of love: deception followed by self-deception followed by loathing followed by self-loathing. He heard himself sigh like an adolescent.

In the cab returning to Fitzhugh Square she stopped talking. Despite whiskey, wine, and brandy she was never more than half-drunk; she never wavered in her erect swooping carriage nor slurred a syllable of her speech. But when he caught a glimpse of her face in the neon from Shaftesbury Avenue, her expression was weary and wretched; she looked as if she sat alone in some featureless place beyond alcohol and anger. He took her hand, which stiffened and then relaxed. To his surprise he understood that he would sleep in the old bed again.

When they reached her living room, still silent, he embraced her. She held him close but turned her face away. He heard himself say again, "Let's go to bed."

She shook her head. "I won't do that," she said. "Richard returns tomorrow or the day after and I should have to tell him, which would be disagreeable."

Suddenly he felt tired, middle-aged, almost relieved that she would not have him. Then she added, "Don't go. I don't want you to go. Taxis are difficult at this hour. Stay with me. However, there will be no reminiscing."

No, he would find a taxi. She became urgent, and her urgency almost raised his spirits, but he remained silent.

"Then at least you must tuck me up," she said.

She swept into the bathroom carrying a robe and when she emerged ready for bed she had composed a sentence. "It is an aging and not altogether attractive body."

She crept under the covers of the bed he remembered and he smoothed the comforter over her long body. She had removed her makeup, which left her looking older, pale, and more beautiful. He felt a surge of old feeling but with it came a note to assure him that it was not new feeling.

"Once more." She spoke like an actress again. "I would like you to stay. I do not want you to leave but you cannot stay except under the circumstances that I insist upon. If you must leave I will call a taxi, but I wish you to stay."

He looked down at her under the covers and shook his head. She dialed a number, but when he saw the misery on her face, he reached down to the telephone and cut off her call. Taking off his clothes he crawled into bed beside her. Immediately he was aroused and poked at her, but she shook her great head, closed her eyes, and lay on her back like a catafalque in a Norfolk church. Three times during the night he woke and rolled over to her, but she remained adamant. When light woke him in the morning, he remembered how, in a dialogue of Plato's, Alcibiades said that he rose from the bed of Socrates "as from the couch of a father or an elder brother."

Wearily he stood to dress, knowing that he would not fall asleep again. He looked down at Rosalind's sculptural body under swathed bedclothes in light that narrowly edged the shades. With another sigh he rejected his allusion; she was neither father nor brother, mother nor young sister: His old love was angry, although she was not only angry. Pulling the shade aside he glanced down at early morning crowds pushing toward the Fitzhugh Square tube—hundreds of them, secretaries still wearing minis, clerks uniform with rolled umbrellas. The sight of them, so purposive and nervous, filled him with irritation: If they were interchangeable parts, then he was interchangeable also. Directly underneath the window an old woman hawked newspapers by a scrawled poster: SCARGILL TO MAGGIE: NO. Then she rolled her scarved head back, looking directly up at him, their eyes catching for a moment. To his surprise he saw that she was weeping, her face red with tears. He turned abruptly away, to find Rosalind's dark eyes open, wide against her pale face and faintly lavender bedclothes. "I shall boil you an egg," she said.

ARGUMENT

AND

PERSUASION

I.

A husband and wife named Raoul and Marie lived in a house beside a river next to a forest. One afternoon Raoul told Marie that he had to travel to Paris overnight on business. As soon as he left, Marie paid the Ferryman one franc to row her across the river to the house of her lover Pierre. Marie and Pierre made love all night. Just before dawn, Marie dressed to go home, to be sure that she arrived before Raoul returned. When she reached the Ferryman, she discovered that she had ne-glected to bring a second franc for her return journey. She asked the Ferryman to trust her; she would pay him back. He refused: A rule is a rule, he said.

If she walked north by the river she could cross it on a bridge, but between the bridge and her house a Murderer lived in the forest and killed anybody who entered. So Marie re-turned to Pierre's house to wake him and borrow a franc. She found the door locked; she banged on it; she shouted as loud as she could; she threw pebbles against Pierre's bedroom windows. Pierre awoke hearing her but he was tired and did not want to get out of bed. "Women!" he thought. "Once you give in, they take advantage of you. . . ." Pierre went back to sleep.

Marie returned to the Ferryman: She would give him *ten* francs by midmorning. He refused to break the rules of his job; they told him cash only; he did what they told him. . . . Marie returned to Pierre, with the same lack of result, as the sun started to rise.

Desperate, she ran north along the riverbank, crossed the bridge, and entered the Murderer's forest.

2.

At 9:00 A.M. on a cool April morning, seventeen young women sat in plastic classroom chairs, each with a paddle-shaped writing surface. When Dr. Silva finished telling the story, he paused until the girls stopped their note-taking and looked up at him. He smiled as he had smiled in a hundred other composition classes when he had told about Raoul and Marie. He continued: "This is not a trick story. There is no *correct* answer, but for forty minutes, please argue an answer to the question: Which of the characters in this story is morally most responsible for Marie's death?"

He wrote the question on the board and turned back to the class. "This impromptu gives you the opportunity to shape an argument. Be logical. In the next five minutes you may ask questions. There will be no further questions after five minutes are up. Do your thinking now." Myra Bobnick was already writing. "Do not start writing your impromptu before you have thought it out." Myra raced into her second page as if there were a contest for the most pages. Helen DeVane looked puzzled as ever and put her hand up. "I will list and spell all names on the blackboard," Dr. Silva said; he wrote:

Raoul

Marie

Ferryman

Pierre

Murderer

When he finished he nodded in Helen's direction.

"Did like this really happen?"

He could never tell what Helen's question would be, but he knew it would be dull-witted. He also knew that she didn't really want an answer; she wanted only to postpone the moment of writing. When he answered Helen, he feared that he sounded so patient that he revealed his annoyance. "It doesn't matter, Helen. Certainly; why not? But it's just a story, something to write about." She nodded her head but the puzzlement never left her face.

Young women crossed their blue-jeaned legs and addressed the lined pads before them. This class was the first of three on Wednesday. All would do the same impromptu and if some of the later classes heard the story ahead of time, he knew it would make no difference. The girls chewed their fingernails or their Bics, either thinking or trying to look as if they were thinking. Magda had a question. "The ferry guy, did he work for himself, I mean with his own boat?"

"In the story," said Dr. Silva, "he implies that somebody else makes the rules."

There were no more questions. Now he could daydream for half an hour. He enjoyed this moment of English Composition 101, when fifteen or twenty pens scratched in front of him and he could look out the window at the grosbeaks coming to the feeder he had put there. Young female heads bent over paper like so many birds poking for sunflower seed. He checked his class list. There would have been eighteen but Jeanette was still in the infirmary. A year ago they had been graduating seniors in their suburban high schools; now they were freshmen at Connecticut Hills, a two-year college once called a finishing school, where he knew himself fortunate to have a job. He did not write books; for the good jobs you had to write books. Most of his work was three or four sections of English Composition—teaching the art of English prose to girls who could not, most of them, read anything more complicated than the labels of their cashmere sweaters. One term a year he relaxed into a section of the Sophomore Introduction to Great Books, a soft reward for all his labor over comma splices: *The Odyssey*, a touch of Thucydides, *Othello*.

Mary Ellen Budd was walking up to the desk. He shook his head; no questions after five minutes. Mary Ellen looked hopeless, sat down, and wrote nothing for the next ten minutes. He understood: She was demonstrating Dr. Silva's injustice; he also understood that she would get over it.

He could not remember who had told him the story of Raoul and Marie. It was early in graduate school, those happy-go-lucky first three years of marriage and provisional adulthood, in-between time that was also the best time, he often acknowledged, though not out loud; Anne did enough acknowledging out loud, when she had had something to drink. Back then in Ann Arbor someone at a party had told the story; it was supposed to be an anecdote Camus liked to tell, asking: "Who's most to blame?" Arthur Silva had said from the start that he knew the answer even if there wasn't supposed to be one: the Murderer. It made him feel morally clear-sighted to give this answer and defend it.

He looked at the pretty heads bent down before him: children of privilege, growing up rich in America—no brains . . . And when they had brains, which happened at Connecticut Hills more often than you might expect, the brains were well-trained to believe that they were stupid; or to know by an unstated rule that if they wished to remain daughters who were loved, cherished, and protected, they had better *act* stupid.

Bethany had finished her page and a half and checked it over: obedient girl—and not stupid by half. It was Dr. Silva's task, as he saw it, to teach girls like Bethany Adams—not to write sentences, not to employ the major rhetorical patterns, not to write A themes—but: *I am not dumb.* This was his mission at Connecticut Hills, and when he succeeded it was gratifying. He sighed, reminding himself that it was opposite to the lesson that he had learned. After five years in the Ph.D. program at the University of Michigan, with the M.A. behind him and generals twice failed, he had been summoned by the Graduate Faculty Committee and requested to withdraw from the Ph.D. program. Of course they would help him get a job, they assured him, for he was a competent teacher of composition. They apologized that their judgment had failed when they admitted him to the program, but they could not therefore compound the error by permitting him to continue. After he pleaded his case, the textual scholar Waldo Slaughter silenced him with one sentence: "You are not Ph.D. material." The words remained permanently attached to him, as if they were printed on his forehead in diploma-script. He remembered how old Braithewaite kept nodding his head, as if with encouragement, at every devastating generalization.

Oh, to take those words home to Anne, with Joanie only two years old!—Anne who had quit the M.A. program in French to take a job when they married, then quit her job to have Joanie. As it happened, the promised support consisted of a one-year job at an academy outside Detroit. After which, with a certain amount of back-door help from the guiltier senior professors, Arthur Silva had been accepted into the doctoral program of the education department of an old normal school turned state university, and in two years he wore the desired letters after his name.

"Time's up!" he said. "You have an extra minute for checking." Five hours later—two more classes, brown bag lunch, office hours—he bicycled home with fifty-seven impromptus about a murder in a forest in generalized France.

3.

When Raoul returned from Paris at noon he was exhausted and hungry. It annoyed him that Marie was nowhere about. It was unlike her, although she sometimes took a *fin* in the morning with one of her gabby oldwife friends. There was of course her ridiculous *affaire du coeur* with Pierre, about which Raoul pretended convenient ignorance. They had, after all, been married a dozen years. And after all, what was he doing in Paris? He sighed in delicious recollection of a seamstress.

Raoul was too tired to make the rounds of the cafés. He swallowed some stale bread with sweet butter and a slab of cold pink lamb. He read three pages in *L'Encyclopédie* and slept until seven o'clock in the evening. He woke and called Marie's name, intent on complaining about her absence. When she did not answer he was suddenly frightened. Where in hell was Marie?

4.

Thursday was Dr. Silva's day without classes; therefore he let Wednesday be theme-day, and spent all Thursday at the breakfast table, blitzing through a stack of papers with his red pencil and his *Harbrace College Handbook*—a dreadful text, but he knew the symbols for correction so well that they appeared as characters in his dreams. When you had sixty themes on the same subject—Dr. Silva had worked at schools where he taught composition to a hundred students a term—the first twenty went quickly. You began with one or two of the best, to set a measure. You knew who the best would be. After one class meeting, you knew which students would have A's at the end of the term. This knowledge depressed him—what was the purpose of his teaching?—but he used this knowledge. You set the rest against the models, almost like grading on a curve. With a free theme it was harder but he rarely gave free themes anymore. The students complained that they had no ideas; freedom was the last thing they wanted: They wanted to know what he wanted so that they could do what he wanted so that they could receive the C's that they wanted.

Anne brought him a pot of coffee in a thermal jug before she went to work in the travel agency. Familiar sarcasms dropped sleepily from the corner of her mouth. Now that Joanie had finished college and worked in San Francisco, they could survive without her job, and usually her jobs didn't last very long. Usually she was fired for being unpleasant to customers. What people called sarcasm he knew for disappointment. He knew who had let her down, and that was why, as he told himself, he never answered her bitterness with bitterness. Every now and then she was fired for drinking, and if she were home all day— Dr. Silva's teaching schedule was long, with conferences, office hours, and the writing lab on Mondays and Fridays—what would she do with her time but drink? She was holding onto her present job, although her complaints accelerated. One day she would leave work early; one day he would bicycle home to find her sitting with a bottle.

On this Thursday he was more than halfway through by the time Anne came home for lunch. But the remaining themes always took half-again as long, and sometimes he put the last papers off until the next morning, working from six to eight before the nine o'clock class that began his long Friday.

"What's the score?" Anne said as she came in.

"About like last year," he said. He looked at the sheet where he kept tab, four upright marks slanted through to make five. "Marie 20, Pierre 5, Raoul 4, Ferryman 1."

5.

Pierre woke in his house across the river about the time Raoul returned from Paris. The cook who doubled as serving maid brought him brioches and café au lait while he read *Le Monde*.

For a long time he felt slightly ill at ease, as if there were something he had forgotten to do. Twice he checked his calendar, but there was nothing on until teatime. He adjusted his foulard in the mirror and drank more coffee. Then he remembered: That slut Marie had knocked at his door all night! He filled with indignation for the sake of his friend Raoul. Perhaps it was time to give Marie her walking papers, amusing as she had seemed at the beginning. Pierre curled his lip. Pierre sharpened the points of his black mustache.

He allowed himself to think of potential replacements. Perhaps it was time to allow Marguerite the pleasures of his bed. She seemed ready a month ago, and surely Alphonse would be complaisant if not downright grateful. On the other hand there was Sylvie, a touch young perhaps at fifteen, but therefore perhaps amusing. At any rate, he felt certain, there would soon be an opening. These ruminations relieved him of his annoyance and cheered him up. He allowed *la petite bonne*, who was a great-grandmother at forty-seven, to leave when she had cleaned up after lunch, although Rose-Rose was not due until four o'clock.

6.

After lunch Arthur Silva worked until 3:45, when he had to interrupt his day at home. He stood, stretched, unlocked his bike and pumped toward the campus for a special conference with Jeanette, who had been ill for two weeks and required make-up assignments. He enjoyed the break in his day of correcting impromptus, but as he pedaled he could not clear them from his mind. Marie kept getting most of the votes: She should have done this, she should have done that; she was at fault because she forgot to bring her return fare for the Ferryman, because of her taste in rotten Pierre, because she knew that the Murderer was in the forest—and always, implicit if unmentioned, because she was an unfaithful wife.

Tomorrow he would arch his eyebrows and ask Myra Bobnick if she really felt that infidelity was a capital offense? In his ten o'clock, he would ask Ginger Hagstrom about the idea behind her conclusion: "Marie was begging for it." He was not sure that he would raise Mary Ellen Budd's argument in class. It had surprised him a little, for Mary Ellen was only quietly attractive—not heavily made-up, not tightly jeaned—and Mary Ellen had poured scorn upon Marie for her stupidity in not lying her way out of her predicament. Marie was morally responsible for her own death, according to Mary Ellen, because she was so dumb—because after daylight she could have borrowed a franc from practically anybody on Pierre's side of the river, and if Raoul was already back by the time the Ferryman rowed her across, she could just tell him that she had felt like taking a walk after a restless night. Professor Silva sighed for Mary Ellen and for her husbands and lovers; then he sighed for himself and everybody else.

No more lies, thank goodness. Most of the lies happened while Joanie was still little, when he and Anne lurched more than once toward the cliffs of divorce. There had been a long period of calm before Anne's last fling, four years ago at St. Hilda's. And even earlier, he reminded himself, there had been stretches of good time when they had been loyal and kind to each other. He remembered with gratitude the first year of his graduate work at State, when they had joined the Presbyterian Church so that Joanie could go to Sunday School, and to their surprise followed their minister in his clear love of Jesus, whose figure clarified momentarily for both of them and allowed them notions of compassion and grace. But every good memory slid into something bad. That idyll ended when Anne discovered the letters a student of nursing had written Arthur. He could not for the life of him remember how he had allowed himself to ruin their calm by drifting into a casual affair. He remembered only feeling powerless, fated, carried like a chip on the stream.

Deliberately he turned his mind back to the present. Maybe he could write a paper for *College English* about this assignment. He had often thought about it; he had made some notes. He used this impromptu every term when he introduced the subject of Argumentation. It revealed unstated hypotheses, unacknowledged and unexamined; it revealed Logical Fallacies.

Every year a few students named Raoul on the grounds of priority. First, he was a bad husband or Marie would not have been unfaithful; second, since leaving her alone was the earliest fault, it was the most grievous. Few students, in all the years, voted for the Ferryman—because he was only following orders, because his motive seemed less passionate. When they did vote for him, it was on the same grounds: Because his motive seemed least important, mercy would have cost him least; therefore his refusal to transport Marie was capricious, which made him morally most responsible. Dr. Silva rather liked this argument, because he remembered (part of the story told in Ann Arbor) that in France the Ferryman always won the vote: Gallic disgust over the small bureaucrat, *le petit fonctionnaire*. The Ferryman had won Anne's vote, years back in Ann Arbor; she thought it was because she had spent her Junior Year Abroad in France.

Students who found Pierre guiltiest usually showed the most illogic—and they were the sweetest students, unsophisticated believers in romantic love. He could imagine how cynical Mary Ellen Budd would be about such arguments: We could use her, during the class meeting, to argue with the illogic of romantic outrage. The question of greater culpability—he would explain after Mary Ellen had made the point unclearly—is not the same as the question of foulness of character. Similarly, of course, he could find another student to rebut Mary Ellen's equation of Marie's moral culpability with Marie's disinclination to lie.

He smiled with fondness as he remembered how Joanie, who was only sixteen when he told her the story, had turned furious at Pierre. It was in the living room of the dormitory apartment at St. Hilda's, while Anne was still sober and faithful and Joanie a devoted daughter, when things for a while went well. He had never known Joanie so outraged, as he gently questioned her premises. But it had turned sour. Anne's sarcasm sent Joanie in a rage to her room, as a few years later it sent her across the continent to San Francisco.

Dr. Silva pushed uphill toward the bicycle rack. Every pleasant memory started a rabbit that, when it found its hole, found sour defeat. He tried remembering how lucky he was, in his job at Connecticut Hills, but it made him remember how St. Hilda's was good for two years only; then it became a job he left on his own initiative, because Anne carried on with the famously philandering bursar and humiliated Arthur, showing affection to her lover even in public, even at a Christmas party with students. That January in his classroom he had found a map rolled down in front of his blackboard and when he zipped it up had read: DR. SILVA IS A WIMP.

But nobody voted for the Murderer. He locked his bike, walking to his office. Once half a dozen years ago, at St. Hilda's as a matter of fact, a freshman intellectual turned up in his class. Clearly the system had failed. When she advanced her theory that the person who committed the crime was the most responsible for the crime, the class unanimously proclaimed that she was crazy. If you were a murderer, murder was part of the job description, wasn't it?

7.

The Ferryman rode his bicycle home at 8:00 A.M. after his twelve-hour stint. The daytime help had showed up on time for once. His wife bustled at the stove, flour whitening her arms up to her elbows—fat, ugly, and agreeable.

"How'd it go?" she said. "Much work?"

He hung his beret on a peg and slouched to the table yawning. "Seventeen trips. Seventeen francs. What's for dinner?"

"Oeufs à la Russe, truite au beurre, Chateaubriand (bleu, d'accord), pommes frites, Bruxelles, salade verte, and Napoleon. Somebody go just one way?"

With his mouth full of egg and mayonnaise, he took a moment to answer. "That slut with the brown curls who screws around with that fruit on the other side of the river when her husband visits his whore in Paris. Can you beat it? She didn't bring money for the ride back!"

His wife turned the steak in the skillet, stirred the sprouts, and drained the potatoes. "What did she do, try the forest?"

"Hey, how do I know? No skin off my ass. *Tant pis. Merde alors.* People get what's coming to them. When they call your number, your number's up. The bullet's got your name on it, you're dead. The moving finger writes. Rules are rules. I was only following orders."

She served the salad. "You always were a bunghole, honey," she said.

8.

Although he was two minutes early, Jeanette was waiting in her baggy jeans and sweatshirt outside his office, looking pale and anxious as she always did.

"Sorry if I'm late," said Dr. Silva. He made a mental note that his feeder was empty outside his classroom next door; he would bring sunflower seed in the morning. When Jeanette sat down and took out her notebook he asked if she felt able to undertake her make-up work. She nodded, poised with pen and notebook. Dr. Silva read from his class schedule, first the reading assignments, then last week's theme—a three-hundred-word essay using a rhetorical pattern and keyed to a reading assignment. Could she finish this theme in the next ten days? Jeanette nodded.

Then he told her that beginning tomorrow the class hour would be devoted to Argumentation. He asked her if she could spend forty minutes, tonight, writing something like an impromptu—he smiled as he said he trusted her not to spend more than forty minutes—and bring it to class tomorrow. If she could do the latest thing first, he explained, she would be ready to keep up with the classwork—and she could catch up on the old work as she was able. He was conscious again that he was an easy and generous teacher, as he intended to be.

Jeanette thought she could manage, and Dr. Silva for the nth time in his life told the story of Raoul and Marie. Coming to the part where Marie was refused a second time by the Ferryman, and a second time by Pierre, he hurried because Jeanette turned pale until she looked the color of a rainy day. Before he could finish she vomited over his desk.

With a secretary's help, and with the help of another student waiting outside another office, Dr. Silva walked Jeanette to the college infirmary although she whimpered that she did not want to return.

When she was put to bed and sedated he paused by the desk of the head nurse, Mrs. Williams. He asked what Jeanette's illness had been. Mrs. Williams was surprised that he did not know, although they tried to keep such things quiet. After a pause for discretion's sake, she told him: Jeanette had visited a boy's college on a blind date, got drunk, and fraternity boys gang-raped her. She was doing quite well, the nurse told him;

the school psychologist was reassuring, although this relapse would trouble him. . . .

Something like this happened *every year*, Mrs. Williams said, at the same place more often than not. Those fraternities should be abolished! But for all the warnings every autumn— deans and housemothers and seniors—something like this happened almost *every year*. Mrs. Williams shook her head. Tears filled her eyes. Tears filled Dr. Silva's eyes also; shame started in him. Mrs. Williams pulled herself together and ac- knowledged that the girls, even those most brutalized, by and large *survived*. She could mention, but she wouldn't, one or two prominent alumnae who had endured something like Jean- ette's humiliation. . . .

Dr. Silva knew that his face was a bright red as he returned to his office and with paper towels from the washroom cleaned up vomit. He left the window open six inches and bicycled home. Maybe this would be a good night for going to the movies, he thought. He remembered that there was a western at the shopping mall. He and Anne liked westerns, with their clear, simplified morality. Anne had picked up a taste for them during her year in France, where the Parisian critics were mak- ing much of them. But he found her already ironical with her second whiskey, smoking Camel after Camel between yellowed fingers, her grayed hair straggling and her face smudged. Dr. Silva recognized marks of boredom and self-loathing. He poured himself a drink and threw it away. He could not speak to Anne, not now when she had been drinking. His mind kept giving him one excuse: How could he have known? The ex- cuse did not help; when he looked at the papers left to be cor- rected he felt revulsion. "I guess I'll do them in the morning," he said as if to Anne.

"What else is new?" she said.

All night he was restless with guilty and defensive thoughts. He would no sooner fall asleep than Anne would snore and wake him. He turned her gently onto her side and lay still, awake and miserable. At six o'clock he made a pot of coffee and settled down to correct the last dozen themes mechanically. He wrote in the margins, "Is this a capital offense?" with the same mild irony that he had used yesterday and twenty years earlier.

When Anne woke up at seven-thirty he had finished the papers and made more coffee. His mind wandered while "Good Morning, America" talked about famine in Ethiopia, a plane crash in Russia, Princess Di's pregnancy, an Iranian boat capsizing, the execution of a crazed killer in Florida, a high pressure zone over the East, and Wayne Gretzky's hat trick. He bicycled to his nine o'clock class trembling and uncertain, as if he were meeting his first class twenty-five years ago.

9.

When the nighttime Ferryman came back to work at 8:00 P.M., fresh from breakfast, Raoul and Pierre waited for him. Raoul asked questions and the Ferryman answered them defiantly, making the point that rules are rules and he was only following orders. At this last remark Pierre spat in the dust at his feet, then twirled the ends of his mustache. The two men stared at each other. Doubtless Pierre had been less than forthright in recounting his own behavior the previous night, and therefore showed contempt for the Ferryman's petty rigidity. Raoul remained cool as he watched the confrontation.

Then he interrupted, "OK," he said. "She must have gone into the forest. What are we going to do?"

"*Merde alors*," said the Ferryman. "I'm on duty."

Pierre supplied a solution. "Let's all go to sleep," he said. "She's probably just hanging around somewhere. With a friend. Have you tried the saloon? If she isn't back by tomorrow, maybe we ought to call the sheriff."

Raoul turned suddenly bitter. "And then some liberal judge will put the Murderer in an insane asylum. I say we raise a posse."

Pierre said he'd drink to that, and the Ferryman jumped up and yodeled. "Well, I'll be hornswoggled," he declared, slapping his ten-gallon hat against his thigh. "Heh, heh, heh," he croaked, banging his friend Pierre on the back. "I reckon we just got ourselves invited to A NECKTIE PARTY!"

10.

Dr. Silva waited until the seventeen young female bodies, sleepy in their sweaters at nine o'clock, gathered before him. It was Jeanette's class and to his relief she was not there. He realized as he waited for quiet that all the young women in his classes had known about Jeanette's assault from the day it happened. When he had told the story day before yesterday, what could they have thought?

They watched him take the elastic off the papers and quieted down, looking up at him expectantly.

"It was Marie, wasn't it?" said Helen DeVane, followed by a small cheer from most of the class.

"Now I told you that there was no correct answer," he said, "but, yes, you agreed as a class that Marie's moral responsibility was the greatest." He read from his tally sheet for the 9:00 A.M. class: "Marie 14, Raoul 2, Pierre 1."

Girls applauded. It was the game-side of this assignment that made it effective. Today it disturbed him and he spoke almost as if he were cross: "But the point is your arguments. Remember, we are studying Argumentation. I am sure that you all spent last night rereading Chapter Eight of *Writing Well*, 'Argument and Persuasion.' Magda, tell us why Marie was the most responsible?"

Magda put down an unlit cigarette. "Because she cheated on

her husband is why. I mean, if she hadn't cheated it would never have happened?"

Bethany Adams was pumping her arm. He nodded in her direction. "But if her husband hadn't gone off and left her it wouldn't have happened in the first place, or if the Ferryboat guy had trusted her. I say Raoul because he *started* it by going away, because he was the *first*."

Deriding voices defended Raoul from the charge, and said the Ferryman had the *least* to do with it . . . He heard a voice proclaiming Pierre. "Pearl?" he said.

"Yeah," she said, "Pierre did it, I mean he's the worst, you know? I mean there they are, you know, doing it all night and he won't even open the door for her when she's screaming and crying? What a rat."

At this point the class erupted with laughter and argument. It always happened so—and this year he did not want it to happen. He let them shout for a moment, out of control, as the Marie-majority poured scorn on the rest. After a moment he waved his hands for silence. In desperation he tried playing the old tape: "Helen," he said, "you said Marie was guilty for her own death because she had committed adultery. Does anyone find anything to criticize in Helen's logic?" No one spoke.

"You all know what logic is; you all read the chapter." More silence. "Helen, do you think that adultery should be punished?"

Helen lit a cigarette and looked as if she felt picked on.

Dr. Silva continued: "Do you think adultery should be punished by death?" Looking out the window he realized: He had forgotten to bring sunflower seed.

After a sullen moment Barbie Hawkes put up her hand. Dr. Silva nodded, feeling his stomach tremble. "But, I know," she said, "but she really was asking for it, you've got to admit, right?" Dr. Silva's nausea rose as he watched the girls in front of him nod their heads in sage agreement. "She was a dope," somebody said, and through the noise of general agreement he heard Mary Ellen laughing as she described the ways in which Marie could have lied her way out. Somebody's voice, louder than the rest, summed it all up: "She got what was coming to her." Dr. Silva stared at the floor, no longer listening. After a moment the class quieted, as if they felt that they had assumed an authority that wasn't theirs. Silence forced Dr. Silva to speak.

"I wonder," he said, "if any of you gave thought to the notion that the guiltiest person might be the Murderer."

When in earlier years he had made this suggestion, his class usually erupted into a hubbub of derision that he gradually tamed by argument. This time, when he spoke, he caused no hubbub. Someone said "awww," but the sentiment drifted away unconfirmed. As he looked from face to face, the girls lowered their eyes. They were embarrassed, and at first he did not know why. Then Bethany Adams took pity. "I thought about him," she said, "but then I decided: If he's just a Murderer, if that's all he is, then he must be crazy, and if you're crazy how can you be guilty?"

Dr. Silva spoke gently, reaching back to old words because he didn't know how to speak new ones. "You're making an assumption," he said. "The story doesn't say the Murderer is crazy. The story says someone murders people who come through the woods. Haven't we convicted and executed people who did that? Multiple murderers? Haven't we called them guilty? If murdering is crazy, then, by your logic, are all murderers innocent?"

There might be a number of answers to that one, he knew; of course, as he often said to Anne after he had stated a conviction, he didn't mean that he was *right*. . . . He felt his face grow red; he felt his heart pound; he did not want to speak the old words. "You made another assumption," he said. "You said that you 'thought about him.' Do you see why that's an assumption?"

Bethany shook her head. Dr. Silva went on, "How do you know that the Murderer is a man?"

Bethany's face showed a quick glint of intelligence. At the same time, Dr. Silva became aware of a sound from the rest of the room like air escaping from a tire, a collective sigh that expressed mild boredom and mild disgust. He looked at the faces —Mary Ellen, Magda, Pearl, Barbie, Helen, Joan, Tracy, Stacy, Myra, Susan, Kimberly, Hulda, Bethany . . . Pretty faces, most of them, parentally cherished faces of young American women. Mostly they looked at him, he realized, with contempt—or if it was not so strong as contempt it was condescension: *Dr. Silva is a Wimp.* They knew what men do and what women do to outwit or evade what men do. They were sorry for him or contemptuous of him because he did not know.

Suddenly he heard himself plead: "*Please* don't accept this! You don't have to accept this! You think it's all right that Marie got murdered. You think it's *natural.* Why do you think you have to put up with this? Why don't you. . . ?"

He stopped short of mentioning Jeanette, and he did not know what to say next. He did not know what they should do.

11.

As soon as Marie entered the forest she heard footsteps behind her. When she entered the clearing she turned about quickly to face him. He showed no hesitation but emerged from the underbrush to face her in the grassy opening gradually lightening with dawn. He was dressed like a clerk from the Second Empire, or like the emperor himself, with a derby set squarely on his head, a small mustache, and a pince-nez that made his eyes look narrow. He wore clean gray gloves and carried an umbrella.

Marie: I take it that you are the Murderer.

Murderer: I take it that you are my next victim, since you have voluntarily entered the forest that is my domain.

Marie: If you wish it I shall be your next victim. I do, however, question your use of the word "voluntarily," or the idea implicit in the word.

Murderer: You are well-spoken.

Marie: I enter the forest not voluntarily but under compulsion because of the action, inaction, and potential action of three men. You are the fourth man.

Murderer: In your opinion, is the compulsion singular or plural? I speak of course in metaphor. Are we four men, one man, or all men?

Marie: Speaking historically, you are one man. But one or many, your violence is not requisite. It is within the power of your will to commit not murder but mercy.

Murderer: For what reason would I spare your life when I have spared no one else's?

Marie: By sparing my life you proclaim your freedom. Are you an automaton, able only to perform according to rote?

Murderer: And if I spared you, how would it affect my reputation? It would be taken as a sign of weakness. Your fear recognizes my power, which neighborhood anxiety confirms.

Marie: On the contrary, mercy would prove your power and your strength. What power resides in the predictable?

Murderer: A deal of power resides in the predictable—unless and until power shows itself mutable, capricious, whimsical. . . . Invariable obligation, not to say routine, sustains my omnipotence.

Marie: And in your inflexibility you make danger for yourself. If you showed mercy on occasion, your neighbors could allow themselves hope in connection with your power and your forest.

Murderer: A moderate acquaintance with human history makes evident: *Power's use is ineluctable.* Allow me to ask: From what does my power derive?

Marie: From physical strength.

Murderer: From what do your concepts of pity and compassion derive?

Marie: From my physical weakness, or from slave-morality, if you will; you are indebted to the insane philosopher Nietzsche. Jesus had a number of things to say about weakness and strength.

Murderer: Jesus, I need hardly inform you, bred no progeny. Remarkable indeed for moral suggestions and personal behavior, he did not disturb the characteristics of the double helix. Although we may differ on the etiology of ethics, you will agree that ideas are acquired characteristics that do not alter the gene pool.

Marie: The dove descended.

Murderer: And quickened one womb. In order to rid the woods of murderers, the Holy Ghost—possibly in the form of gene-altering radiation—must descend with regularity, must perhaps quicken every womb for three generations. I kill you for the reason that you understand, that you even accept: I am stronger than you are.

Marie: It is my part to tell you: When you kill me because you are stronger than I am, the politics of this murder is only incidentally sexual or I should say physiological—an incidence, naturally enough, that I find poignant—for you authorize your own murder, on the same principle of strength, as soon as a younger or more muscular or more determined Murderer enters the woods. Or a lynch mob, which is your body multiplied by other bodies both weak and strong.

Murderer: Well understood. Are we ready, can-be, for to begin?

Marie: "Let my cry come into Thee."

12.

Dr. Silva canceled his classes and bicycled back to the apartment. He lay on the bed with his head whirling, nauseated when he closed his eyes, desperately tired when he kept them open. After a while he heard Anne come home for lunch, fix a tuna fish sandwich, watch part of a game show, and return to work. With the shades still drawn in the bedroom he lay on his back looking at the ceiling without making a sound until she was gone. Then he rose and paced, bedroom through living room to kitchen and back again. On one of his passes he chewed a sprig of celery; later he ate a handful of bologna and heated bitter coffee.

By the time Anne returned at five-thirty he had made a decision. On Monday, he said, he would submit his resignation to the dean of Connecticut Hills. Over the weekend he would update his curriculum vitae and draft a letter seeking employment. By the end of next week he would have written every community college in California, maybe four-year schools as well—but California's community colleges were famous. Wherever they wound up, he said while Anne nodded, they would be closer to Joanie.

Anne drank Dubonnet slowly while Arthur daydreamed aloud, growing more enthusiastic as his plans turned more concrete. When he paused Anne was agreeable: They should see the country before they got too old; maybe after a few years in California they could take early retirement; maybe they should think again about a trailer in Arizona; maybe she should return to school; maybe she should go into social work, as she had often thought.

By the time they went to bed that evening, Dr. Silva had almost forgotten his shame. Then he remembered: He would have to find a new way to introduce Argument and Persuasion. He had the notion again, which he usually dismissed quickly: Maybe it was time to leave teaching. But what could he do instead? He smiled sleepily thinking: I could be rich. When he was a child he had wanted a car as long as a Pullman. He dove toward sleep remembering a Pierce Arrow that parked on Thursdays when he was a small boy in front of his father's grocery. The chauffeur teased him gently while the old lady went inside to feel the vegetables. His mother told him that he could not be a chauffeur because he was not black. When he said that then he wanted to be a widow, because he knew that Archibald's boss was a widow, his mother repeated his remark all week to everyone who came into the store.

Design by David Bullen
Typeset in Mergenthaler Bembo
by Wilsted & Taylor
Printed by Haddon Craftsmen
on acid-free paper